"Luc, where have you been?" Sophie's voice was barely a whisper. "I've missed you."

His mouth went dry. As he searched for the words, she reached out and ran a gentle finger along his jaw line.

His head tilted into her touch. He wanted to keep her here. Safe.

Her mouth was just a breath from his. Those lips... so tempting...would taste so sweet. A rush of desire urged him to give in to the taste and feel of her while the rest of the world melted away.

There were so many reasons he shouldn't...

...but at the moment, he couldn't seem to remember any of them.

Dear Reader,

At one time or another, most little girls dream of being a princess. Sometime before they hit the teenage years that innocent fantasy gives way to reality. That's how it happened for my heroine Sophie Baldwin, who decided early in life she didn't need a crown to make a difference. Still, somewhere along the way, her drive to change the world became an uphill battle. Thank goodness a twist of fate and a gorgeous man named Luc Lejardin helped her realize life held all sorts of possibilities.

I'm a firm believer that each woman should hold on to the princess dream. Even if we're not of royal blood, each of us is unique and special in our own way. In celebration of that, please take time to honor your inner princess by doing something that makes you happy. Be sure to visit my Web site at NancyRobardsThompson.com and tell me what you did. I love to hear from you!

Warmly,

Nancy Robards Thompson

ACCIDENTAL PRINCESS

NANCY ROBARDS THOMPSON

SPECIAL EDITION

Published by Silhouette Books

America's Publisher of Contemporary Romance

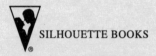 **SILHOUETTE BOOKS**

ISBN-13: 978-0-373-24931-2
ISBN-10:   0-373-24931-4

ACCIDENTAL PRINCESS

Copyright © 2008 by Nancy Robards Thompson

Visit Silhouette Books at www.eHarlequin.com

Printed in U.S.A.

NANCY ROBARDS THOMPSON

Award-winning author Nancy Robards Thompson is a sister, wife and mother who has lived the majority of her life south of the Mason-Dixon line. As the oldest sibling, she reveled in her ability to make her brother laugh at inappropriate moments, and she soon learned she could get away with it by proclaiming, "What? I wasn't doing anything." It's no wonder that upon graduating from college with a degree in journalism, she discovered that reporting "just the facts" bored her silly. Since hanging up her press pass to write novels full-time, critics have deemed her books "funny, smart and observant." She loves chocolate, champagne, cats and art (though not necessarily in that order). When she's not writing, she enjoys spending time with her family, reading, hiking and doing yoga.

This book is dedicated to Jennifer.
Never forget you're a princess.

Prologue

Once upon a time in the days of old (1975), in a kingdom far, far away (an independent island off the coast of France), there was a very naughty teenage *princesse* who had a penchant for very bad boys. She fell in love with a wild rock star and became pregnant out of wedlock. Before the *princesse* told the rock star of her situation, she entrusted the news to her chambermaid, who promptly informed the queen, who in turn informed the king.

The king was furious because he did not think the rock star suitable for his royal daughter. To avoid a scandal, the king sent the *princesse* away against her will to have the baby in secret. Immediately after the birth, the baby was secreted away. Only the king knew the whereabouts of the child.

Something inside the *princesse* changed after giving birth. Haunted by the baby girl she'd never held, she determined that she would get her baby back. When she was free of her father's imprisonment, she got in touch with her beloved rock star, who had been devastated by her disappearance. During the time without her he, too, had changed his wild ways because he knew that the *princesse* was his one true love. He was overcome with a mixture of joy and sadness when he learned of the baby and how the child was taken from his beloved. He immediately dropped down on one knee and vowed to make the young *princesse* his bride and reunite their small family.

However, on the dark and stormy night when the *princesse* and the rock star set out to start their life together, there was a terrible accident. The plane in which they were flying crashed, and much to everyone's sadness, the *princesse* and the rock star perished in the disaster before they could reclaim their child.

Chapter One

"Is everything in place?" Luc Lejardin rose from his antique desk and paced the length of the wooden floor to the arched office window. Expecting an affirmative, he watched the setting sun cast an impressionistic glow over the Mediterranean Sea, reflecting the colored lights of St. Michel as brightly as the crown jewels.

The American on the other end of the line hesitated a split-second too long. "Not quite. I'm close, though."

Lejardin frowned. Most wouldn't have picked up on the nearly imperceptible uncertainty in the speaker's voice. But Luc had. That was his job. To detect lies, disloyalty, duplicity. A human polygraph, as he liked to think of himself.

He trusted no one. Especially now when, for the sake of national security, everything must go without a hitch. There was no room for error on this mission. Not in the wake of the tragedy.

A tragedy he'd failed to prevent.

"I'm not pleased, *monsieur*," Lejardin snapped. "We arrive stateside in less than ten hours. I trust you will have completed your job before we board the plane. If there is a problem, I will assign someone more capable."

"There is no problem," the deep voice assured him. "I'll e-mail the last of the photos to you within the hour."

Luc terminated the call and tucked his Blackberry into the breast pocket of his Armani suit. Underneath the fine fabric, his heart felt heavy. He leaned against the wooden window frame and closed his eyes out of respect for the grieving king and those who'd lost their lives.

The tragic fire that killed Prince Antoine and his family had happened under Luc's watch. Not directly, as Prince Antoine had his own team of Royal Service Agents—agents who worked for Lejardin.

Those men had perished in the fire, too.

As minister of protocol, the blood of those who died would forever remain on Luc's hands. It was something for which he would never forgive himself, despite how King Bertrand insisted there was no way Lejardin could've prevented it.

Refusing to believe that someone was responsible for the tragedy that had stolen what remained of his family, the king clung hard and fast to the belief that the House of Founteneau was cursed. Sometimes Lejardin's most challenging job was protecting the king from himself.

Then the curse had struck again.

Ah, but Luc knew better. He was too much of a realist to believe in curses or anything so far beyond his control. A murderer was behind this tragedy—and most certainly the other deaths that had happened one by one over the past thirty-three years. Each carefully orchestrated to look like an accident. Someone had taken enough care so that even the Crown Council and Luc's own father, who had been minister of protocol until the day he died three years ago and Luc stepped up to the post, had ruled each of the tragedies an accident.

With this "accident," every one of King Bertrand's children, every known Founteneau heir to the St. Michel throne was dead—each perishing in separate, but equally tragic, "accidents."

That one family would endure so much loss was almost unfathomable. Whether he had the king and the Crown Council behind him or not, Luc would not rest until the responsible parties paid for the innocent lives they'd taken.

In the meantime, though, he had other pressing business: ensuring the safety of the only remaining heir to the St. Michel throne. An heir who until yesterday nobody except King Bertrand knew existed.

Sophie Baldwin could've lied to herself and claimed the dress in the window of Tina's boutique was what stopped her dead in her tracks on that cold, gray late-November morning.

Right. As if she'd window shop in downtown Trevard, North Carolina, when she was late for work—again. Not to mention freezing due to the arctic temperatures.

No. It wasn't the dress that had stopped her.

As she walked, she'd glanced enticingly at her reflection, expecting to see the slim, attractive, young woman who lived in her mind's eye, but instead what smiled back at her made her stop and bite back a startled oath—

"What the h…?" She moved closer for a better look. But it was no optical illusion. Bundled up in her big, canary-yellow wool coat, she really did resemble a life-sized squeeze bottle of FRENCH'S Classic Yellow Mustard.

It was startling, really, seeing herself like that. As she assessed the grotesque image, she realized it wasn't just the coat that made her look dumpy. Her brown hair was flat and lank, her green eyes were bloodshot and puffy. She looked haggard, worried and miserable. Much too old and tired for thirty-three.

As people flowed by on the sidewalk, she reached out and touched the weary reflection in the glass. Standing palm to cold palm with this alien, she tried to pinpoint when this dramatic shift had happened and why, until now, she hadn't seen it.

Of course she'd been so busy trying to stay afloat since the divorce that she didn't have time for spa day at the Red Door. Not that she went to the spa regularly predivorce. Come to think of it, Trevard didn't even have a Red Door…unless you counted the one at the entrance to Cheap Tilly's Bargain Barn, but that was about as far away from the Red Door as you could get.

Still, spa or no spa, once upon a time, Sophie Baldwin had been quite a catch. And then she'd turned to mustard. Because don't they say that the outside is simply a reflection of what you are on the inside? Obviously she wasn't even the exotic, spicy variety of mustard. Nope. Just plain-old bland water and vinegar with a few generic spices thrown in to make it palatable. Barely.

Sophie sighed. Yeah, once upon a time men noticed her. Really, they did. It didn't seem so long ago, either. She was a different person then—someone who wouldn't have been caught dead in the hideous mustard coat; someone who laid on the floor to zip herself into skin-tight jeans; someone who would've danced the night away in painfully high stilettos.

Because they would've been sexy stilettos.

And men would've noticed.

But that was when she'd been young and in love and sure that Frank was her Prince Charming and their next stop was happily ever after.

She hadn't fathomed that after fifteen years of marriage and one child together Frank would take a detour to the land of pert, perfect eighteen-year-old bodies.

Shallow idiot, that ex-husband of hers. Ditching his family and shirking his responsibilities to date girls who were just a few years older than his fourteen-year-old daughter.

A gust of cold, wet wind cut through the coat, chilling Sophie to the bone. It was snowing. First flakes of the season. Sophie turned up the yellow collar and held it shut with her gloved hand.

Never mind Frank's midlife crisis. What was going through *her* head when she'd sworn off black and its slimming goodness for *brighter, cheerier* clothes she'd fancied were more representative of her *brighter, cheerier* postdivorce life?

As she tore herself away from the mirror image, she nearly bumped into a woman pushing a toddler in a stroller.

"Oh. I'm sorry," she murmured, realizing the baby was crying. *Screaming.* Tears streaming and snot stringing from her tiny red nose.

For a split second Sophie locked gazes with the young mother, who looked to be in her early twenties. What she saw was both complicated and familiar. On the one hand, she was young and beautiful, the picture of Madonna and child (if the Madonna pushed a stroller); on the other hand, she looked frantic in a how-did-I-lose-control-of-my-life sort of way.

Sophie wanted to tell her, Yes, I was you once. Young and beautiful, owned by a fussy baby, too tired to have sex with my husband…and look at me now.

FRENCH'S mustard on two legs.

By that time the woman had moved on.

Sophie turned off Main Street onto Broad Avenue, quickening her steps toward the social services building. As she walked the remaining two blocks to work, she made a mental note to ban from her wardrobe all colors that resembled condiments…well, except for the coat.

She couldn't do anything rash like dumping it at Goodwill. Not unless she wanted to walk to work in her shirtsleeves in the bone-numbing cold.

She couldn't afford to replace it right now. In fact, she couldn't afford much outside her tight budget, which was one of the reasons she'd chosen to walk the mile and a half to work. Every penny counted right now, and if she could save even a tiny bit by walking, that was an easy sacrifice.

It's just that it had turned so cold.

She snuggled deeper into the ugly coat. At least there were no hotdog vendors in the park in the winter. The chances of someone actually mistaking her for a tubby vat of mustard were slim.

She smiled at the pun, and as she passed the diner, she breathed in the tantalizing scent of bacon, toast and coffee. Her stomach reminded her that she'd been too rushed—again—to eat breakfast. Someday when money wasn't such an issue, she was going to treat herself to a nice, leisurely breakfast before work.

But not today.

As she pulled open the big wooden door of the social services building, it dawned on her that this practical person she'd become must signal that she was in a new life phase.

Being a single mother did tend to push one toward practicality. Gone were the whims and flights of fancy. She'd traded them in for grounding and sensibility because that's what it took to give her daughter, Savannah, the best life possible.

That's what kept Sophie from telling Savannah the ugly truth about the divorce. Despite how Savannah blamed her mother, all Sophie would say was that the matter was a grown-up issue. No matter how much Savannah pushed and needled, Sophie refused to expose the child-support-dodging, two-timing louse who could do no wrong in his little girl's eyes.

Maybe someday when Savannah was grown they'd have that conversation, but not now.

Even if he wasn't forthright in supporting his daughter monetarily because he'd spent the better part of the year "between jobs," he did spend time with Savannah, and the girl needed to cling to that rock when he was in town. She had suffered enough during the divorce.

One of the things that surprised Sophie the most about the ordeal was that she thought working as a social worker would've prepared her for divorce. She'd helped numerous women get back on their feet after their marriages dissolved. Still she'd felt just as alone and scared as the best of them.

At least she had a good job and benefits—that was one of the main reasons she'd decided not to pack up and move to Florida with her parents after Frank left.

The elevator *dinged,* and Sophie waited for three people aboard to exit. Once they did, she stepped inside and gave a cursory glance around the lobby to see if there were others rushing to catch the elevator, too. Nope, she was the only one. She glanced at her watch to see just how late she was and her heart quickened: 8:20.

Twenty minutes. Yikes. Her first appointment wasn't until 8:30. Maybe she'd still be able to slide into her office unnoticed.

She jabbed the third-floor button a few times, as if that would shift the ancient machine into express mode. But the doors stayed open, like a big mouth indulging in a long, lazy yawn.

"Come on." She gave the button another impatient tap. This time the doors slid shut. She hated being late, but sometimes she just couldn't help it. Sometimes she was operating on only three or four hours of sleep after working her second job waiting tables at Bob's Steak House. This was one of those mornings, and it had turned into a comedy of errors that began with a scavenger hunt for a homework assignment Savannah swore she'd left on the table the night before. That prompted Sophie to issue the usual "you need to get everything ready the night before" speech. Which, in turn, elicited eye rolls and sullen *harrumphs* from her daughter.

That she was forced to be the "bad cop" rankled her on so many levels. She was the disciplinarian, while Frank got to ride in on a figurative white horse, like Prince Valiant to the rescue. The cool dad who'd moved to California, gotten a tattoo and had his ears pierced, when Sophie had just vetoed her daughter's request for a belly-button ring.

When the elevator finally reached the third floor and the

doors slid open, Sophie's heart lurched at the sight of her boss, Mary Matthews, standing at the front desk talking to Lindsay Bingham, the receptionist and Sophie's best friend.

Mary, wispy, thin and city chic, stopped midsentence and leveled Sophie with a look, before glancing pointedly at her watch.

"Nice of you to join us." She tucked a strand of sleek, black bob behind an ear. "Sleeping in?"

Luc sipped a glass of sparkling water and opened the thick file on the tray table in front of him. He leafed through the stack of photos he'd received a mere forty-five minutes before boarding the plane. Cutting it a little too close for his liking, but at least the investigator had come through.

He paused at a close-up of Sophie Baldwin's face. There was no denying the woman was attractive, with her engaging smile, shoulder-length dark hair and light green eyes. Though, she wasn't exactly what he'd expected. *Très naturelle.*

Naturally she hadn't been groomed for the role that was about to be thrust upon her. So, really, should there be any expectations?

A little voice inside him that knew far too much piped up, *Oh, but everyone will have expectations. Lofty, unfair ideals that no mere mortal should ever be held to. But she will be. Just as has each of those who've come before her.*

He flipped to the next photo of Sophie on the porch of a modest clapboard house. Then to another of her bundled up in a hideous bright yellow coat, with a large purse slung over her shoulder and a satchel in hand as she walked along a quaint downtown sidewalk; then to yet another shot of her in a market—or grocery store as they called it in the States—

reaching for something on a shelf. In this photo, she wasn't wearing the coat. Her clothes were neat but ordinary, except for how they clung to her voluptuous body, making her curves look rather sexy—

Luc dropped the thought like hot coal. He closed the thick case file with a sharp flick of his wrist, irritated with himself for letting his thoughts stray.

Closing his eyes, he rubbed his throbbing temples.

It was fatigue talking. Yes, that was the reason. He'd barely slept since the accident.

How long had it been now? He'd lost count in the midst of the madness, but it had to have been more than seventy-two hours.

Seventy-two of the worst *damn* hours of his life.

Just three short days ago everything had been normal. Then the world upended and in the blink of an eye everyone in St. Michel was plunged into the nightmare of yet another royal death. The most recent in a long tragic line that began with the loss of Princess Sylvie, who died in 1975 in a plane crash; then Princess Celine lost her life in a car accident eight years later; next Prince Thibault drowned in a 1994 diving disaster; now Prince Antoine and his entire family…wiped out in one fatal blow.

Luc drew in a sharp breath, trying to work through the pain that was as real as if a strong hand twisted his gut.

He hadn't even had a chance to say goodbye.

Antoine was more than the youngest son of his employer. The prince had also been Luc's friend and confidant.

Growing up in the St. Michel palace, he'd played with Antoine as a kid; they'd gone to school together as adolescents and caused their share of heartache with the ladies while away at university. Luc had been with Antoine the night he met Leanna, and stood up with them when they took their marriage vows.

This loss went deeper than anyone could ever understand. Especially since his gut screamed that this—like the other senseless deaths—was no accident.

Luc closed his eyes against the pain—against the fury. The realization came over him in waves that in the midst of the chaos he hadn't had a chance to slow down long enough to grieve the loss of his friend.

The plane dipped through a patch of turbulence. The jolt yanked him back to the present, a safe distance from his despair. Glancing around the cabin at the five dark-suited security agents who'd accompanied him on the mission—each sleeping or reading or otherwise occupied—Luc steeled his resolve and reminded himself of his duty.

He was the minister of protocol.

He set the tone for the mission.

Despite how this loss, this assault on his king and country—on his *best friend*—devastated him, there was no time to let emotion cloud his judgment.

A corner of one of the Sophie Baldwin photos had worked itself out of the folder, as if challenging him to take another look. Luc drew it out and analyzed it with professional eyes.

She looked like a nice woman.

Too bad she'd be dragged into the midst of this mess.

He tucked the photo back into the folder, straightened it so that the contents were aligned and glanced at his watch.

The plane would land stateside in approximately one hour. He and his team would hit the ground running. Luc wanted to be *damn* sure that everyone involved understood the importance of their roles.

Especially Sophie Baldwin.

Mary Matthews drummed her French-manicured nails on the reception desk. Her hardened gaze meandered the length of Sophie's yellow coat.

Under the scrutiny, Sophie shifted her briefcase from one hand to the other. Her mind raced to find a plausible excuse for her tardiness, but she came up at a loss for anything but the truth.

"I'm sorry. I worked at the restaurant last night, and Savannah and I got off to a rough start this morning."

Mary's lip curled.

"Right. Rough starts seem to be part of your morning routine. They happen so frequently."

Sophie took a deep breath, tempted to list all the times that she'd worked late.

"It's just that—"

"Clock in and meet me in my office. Five minutes."

Mary had been Sophie's boss less than a year, joining the Trevard Social Services team just after Sophie filed for divorce. Needless to say Sophie hadn't been herself since she'd met Mary, despite every effort to put her best foot forward. She tried. God knows she tried, but sometimes on mornings like this it seemed next to impossible to get out of her own way, much less get an eighth-grader out the door and to the bus stop on time. Even so, Sophie had a feeling even if everything in her life had been perfect, she and Mary Matthews wouldn't have mixed.

Even though Mary had been a punctuality stickler when she first arrived, she seemed to have lightened up on clock watching over the past few months. Or so Sophie thought.

As she got to her cubicle and stashed her purse in the bottom desk drawer, she wracked her brain, trying to guestimate how many times she'd been tardy lately. Of course all Mary would have to do is pull the time sheets to see when Sophie had punched in.

When Sophie got to Mary's office, she discovered that was exactly what she'd done. The woman nudged a piece of paper with a neat row of dates and numbers running the length of the page.

September 3—fifteen minutes late.

September 5—twenty-five minutes late.

September 10—seventeen minutes late.

And so on…each infraction highlighted in bold fluorescent yellow.

Sophie's cheeks burned. For God's sake, the woman hadn't just printed out a report; she combed through the past year and tallied up each infraction.

How much time had *that* project taken?

"I've warned you, Sophie." Mary sat sunken cheeked and ramrod straight in her chair, her hands folded neatly on the spotless desk blotter. "Time and time again, I've warned you, but you're not taking me seriously, are you?"

"I—"

A simple flutter of Mary's hand silenced Sophie.

"Since you've chosen to ignore me, you leave me no choice but to write you up."

The words slapped Sophie speechless. It was as if her voice had been encapsulated in a soundproof bubble that was lodged in her throat…

Then the bubble popped.

"Mary, I'm sorry if it seems that I've blatantly disregarded your wishes. That certainly wasn't my intention. But I'm sure if you poll my clients and look at my caseload, you'll see my work hasn't suffered even if on occasion I don't punch the clock at eight on the dot. I mean, come on, when I'm late I stay after to make up the time."

Mary's stonewall expression remained impervious.

"Office hours are from 8:00 a.m. until 5:00 p.m. Those are the hours of operation. If I make an exception for you, I have to make exceptions for everyone else. In fact just the other day one of your coworkers asked if she could telecommute for a portion of the day." Mary rolled her eyes. "Of course I had to say no. It would be unfair to refuse her request and then turn around and tolerate your habitual tardiness."

Once again Sophie was speechless, exasperated by her boss's twisted logic.

The rasp of Mary opening her center drawer broke the silence. She pulled out yet another piece of paper and a black pen and slid them across the desk toward Sophie.

"If you'll sign this document acknowledging that I counseled you, we can both get to work."

Sophie stared at the paper as if it would scald her if she touched it. If she didn't, maybe it would self-destruct.

Fat chance.

Then as if someone turned up the heat on the resentment that had been simmering inside her, anger flared. She'd had it up to her eyebrows with documents that demanded her signature. Since the divorce she'd signed so many papers against her will she'd lost count. People telling her what to do, when to do it. That she deserved *nothing* from a divorce she didn't even want. When actually what she wanted was quite simple: She wanted to wake up from this nightmare. She wanted to sit up in her bed, foggy with sleep, breathing a sigh of relief that Frank was beside her. The divorce had all been a bad dream. Her husband wasn't a cheat—he valued their marriage and family as much as she did.

It was a nightmare all right. Only it wasn't anything she could escape.

She looked up at Mary, mustering her best poker face. "And what if I don't sign?"

Mary blinked, sucked in a deep breath as if she was taking a long drink of patience.

"Then I will be forced to note that you…that you *refused*."

Feeling a little dizzy from flirting with defiance, Sophie glanced around Mary's office trying to get her bearings. Her boss had no personal photos in her office. In fact the only things that remotely warmed up the cold, white institutional space were a couple of cheap-looking floral prints slapped on the sterile walls. How could she expect a woman like Mary Matthews to understand? It suddenly washed over Sophie that no matter how bad life seemed right now, at least she *had* a life. She had photos on her desk of a teenage girl who sometimes needed her in the morning and, yes, sometimes caused her to be late and if that was such a crime, well—

Mary's intercom buzzed. "Excuse me, Ms. Matthews?" Lindsay's voice sounded through the speaker. "I'm sorry to bother you, but Sophie has two clients out here waiting to see her. Mr. Carlo, her *first* appointment and um, Laura Hastings, who doesn't have an appointment but says it's important."

Sophie felt vindicated by the way Lindsay had emphasized *first* appointment. She'd obviously made it to work in plenty of time for her clients—and even had a few extra minutes to debate the finer points of punctuality with Mary.

She forced a smile that didn't make it to her eyes. "Well, I'd love to sit and chat all day, but I need to get to work. My 8:30's here."

Sophie stood to go.

"The document," Mary said. "Sign it before you go."

Sophie snatched the paper off the desk and returned Mary's stone-cold gaze. "I never sign anything until I read it."

"Fine. Take it with you, but I expect it on my desk by the end of the day."

As she walked out of Mary's office, Sophie resisted the urge to crumple the unsigned form into a ball. Instead she took a deep breath and did her best to cope with the adrenaline rush, pumped by the argument with Mary.

There was no time for stewing. She had back-to-back client meetings with Laura Hastings added to the mix. She was already behind. She'd get to Mary's form when she could. It might even be this weekend.

As she rounded the corner into the crowded waiting room, Laura stood to greet her. An ambivalent smile pulled at the corners of her lips, but didn't quite reach her sad eyes. The fragile-looking redhead was one of Sophie's favorite clients and proudest success story. This single mother of four had fled an abusive marriage, and with Sophie's help, she'd managed to cross the rickety bridge from welfare checks to being gainfully employed and enrolled at the community college part-time, working toward a nursing degree.

It was a full load, but Laura was the poster child of why Sophie loved her job. Helping people better themselves was the reason she went into social work in the first place. *To make a difference in the world.*

"Laura, good morning." She gave the woman a quick hug. "How are the kids?"

Laura cleared her throat. "Well, that's what I wanted to talk to you about—"

"Excuse me, I have an 8:30 appointment and it's already 8:35." A short, round man who resembled Danny DeVito sidled up to them. "I'm going to be late for work. Can we get this show on the road?"

Sophie looked from Mr. Carlo to Laura, who ducked her head and cleared her throat again.

"Of course," she whispered apologetically, taking a step backward as if retreating into her shell. "I'm sorry. Go right ahead."

"Can you wait?" Sophie asked Laura.

She nodded.

"Sophie there's a call for you on line one," Lindsay said. "Do you want to take it or should I put it through to your voice mail?"

Mr. Carlo threw up his hands. "What's the point of an appointment if everyone else waltzes right in ahead of you?"

At that moment, Mary rounded the corner with her purse on her arm. "Is there a problem?"

Voice mail, please, Sophie mouthed to Lindsay, who in turn mouthed, *Sorry.*

"Yes," said Mr. Carlo, his voice raising several decibels. "I booked an appointment for 8:30 this morning so I'd get right in. Now it's nearly quarter till. I'm going to be late for work because you guys can't get your act together."

Mary arched a brow and shot Sophie a knowing look.

Oh, for God's sake.

"Sophie, take care of the gentleman. Lindsay, I have an appointment at the county building. I'll be out for a couple of hours."

With that, she left.

Yeah, thanks for the help, Mary.

"Mr. Carlo, please have a seat in my office—first door on the left. I'll be right there."

The man didn't budge. "Oh, no, no, no. If I go in there and leave you two out here, you'll yak about the kids all day long. I'll wait right here and walk back with you."

He crossed his arms over his barrel chest and drummed his fingers on his beefy arm.

"I'll…I'll…I can come back," Laura stuttered, edging toward the door. Something was wrong. She only stuttered when she was upset, and Sophie had a feeling she wasn't simply flustered by Mr. Carlo's blustering.

"I won't be long, Laura. Please wait."

But the woman waved her off with an unsteady hand and slipped out the door.

Chapter Two

Sophie's office phone rang as she swallowed the last bite of tuna sandwich. Before the divorce, she used to treat herself to lunch out on Fridays. Sometimes with Lindsay, sometimes by herself. It was always something she looked forward to.

Someday she'd enjoy that indulgence again, she reminded herself as she tossed a piece of used plastic wrap into the trash and answered the call.

"This is Sophie Baldwin."

"Hmm…Mom?"

She glanced at her watch—12:30. The school day wasn't over yet.

"Hi, honey. What's wrong?"

Sophie's mind raced to what she'd say to Mary if she had to leave to pick up a sick child after being late today.

"Oh. My. God. Mom, you need to come home. Right now."

Sophie's heart quickened at the sound of Savannah's panic-laced voice.

"Home? Are you at home?"

Savannah hesitated for a moment.

"Grandma and Grandpa are here. Did you know they were coming? And that they were bringing six creepy men with them?"

"What? Grandma and Grandpa are here? In town? What's going on? Where are you?"

"I said I'm at home, and I have no idea what's going on. That's why I'm calling *you*."

Ah, there it was—the sarcasm that seemed to penetrate every conversation with her daughter these days.

"Did Grandma and Grandpa pick you up from school?"

Silence.

"Savannah, are you there?"

"Yeah."

"Put your grandmother on the phone."

"Well…*hmm*…I can't."

Oh, for heaven's sake. "Why not?"

Another stretch of silence. Sophie wondered if this might be another of Savannah's cries for attention. She'd been pulling stunts since her father left. Nothing horrendously bad, just pushing Sophie's buttons with out-of-character antics such as cutting class and befriending a goth girl—er—*emo* girl, as Savannah had pointedly corrected her. Because goth was so five minutes ago.

Whatever happened to Elmo—the little, lovable, red, fuzzy monster on *Sesame Street* Savannah used to love so much not *that many* years ago?

These emo kids were a far cry from Elmo—they were dark

and scary. Or as Savannah explained, emos were all about *emotion.* That's why Emo Jess had tattooed her boyfriend's name, Tick, across her neck in bold, three-inch letters.

"Savannah, put your grandmother on the phone right now."

The girl sighed—as if all the problems in the world rested on her shoulders. "Grandma asked me not to call you. She said we could talk about this—whatever *this* is—after you got home from work. But something's going on and it's really creeping me out. Will you *please* come home?"

All the fight and sarcasm had left her daughter's voice. She sounded like the sweet predivorce kid Sophie so desperately missed. If her daughter *wanted* her there—

"Okay, sweetie, I'm on my way."

When Sophie got home, the first thought that crossed her mind was the man who met her at the door—the one with the French accent who'd introduced himself as Luc Le-something-or-the-other and maintained eye contact even as he *bowed*—yes, he actually bowed—was the spitting image of the actor Olivier Martinez.

His disarmingly handsome face had the same chiseled cheeks, intense dark eyes that crinkled at the corners when he smiled and a similar aquiline nose above the most gorgeous full lips.

The resemblance was uncanny, and it knocked her for a loop.

For about two seconds.

"What the heck is going on, Mr. Le...?" she demanded. "Why are you in my house?"

Several possibilities crossed her mind: This guy was a repo man concerned about her ex-husband's bad debts or a flimflam man who was trying to take advantage of her elderly parents.

"Luc Lejardin," he repeated, his accent as smooth as butter. "I am here with your parents to discuss with you a matter of great importance."

Knowing her parents, it was more likely to be an Amway sales pitch than a home invasion. Still, a single mother couldn't be too careful.

Sophie clutched the cell phone in her coat pocket. The situation didn't seem dangerous, but if anything changed, all she had to do was call 911. Her index finger traced the numbers as she pushed past Olivier—er Luc, or whatever his name was—through the foyer and into the living room.

There were five more men in there dressed in somber dark suits, looking like they'd stepped out of a scene from *Men in Black*. And there were her parents, Rose and John Jones, perched sheepishly on the edge of the chintz sofa, looking not the least bit frightened, but definitely a tad surprised to see her.

"Sophie, *ma chérie*." Her mother stood, and her father, a man of few words, followed stiffly. "Are you home for lunch?"

Sophie narrowed her eyes.

"No, I was eating my lunch when Savannah called to tell me you and your...*friends* had dropped by. *All the way from Florida, no less.*"

Her mother shook her head and scowled. "I told her not to bother you at work." Her French accent was more pronounced than usual. That always happened when she was flustered. "This really could have waited until you got home." She hugged Sophie and gave her a quick kiss on each cheek.

"By the way, why was Savannah home from school today?" Rose wagged her finger. "If she was sick, she shouldn't have friends over. She especially shouldn't be alone in the house with a boy."

What?

"Savannah didn't stay home sick today." Sophie narrowed her eyes at her mother. "You and Dad didn't pick her up from school on your way in?"

They did that sometimes.

But her parents shook their heads.

The slow burn simmered in her belly and she felt like maybe she'd caught *someone* trying to pull a fast one.

"Where is Savannah?" she asked.

"In her room."

She'd deal with her daughter later. "Good. While she's in there, you can tell me what's going on."

A deer-in-headlights expression swept over Rose's face. "Well, *ma chérie,* it's a long, complicated story."

Rose lowered herself onto the couch. John did the same. Her parents looked at each other as if deciding who would speak first.

"I don't even know where to begin." Rose shot Luc a pleading look.

"Madame, allow me." Luc turned to Sophie. "I'm sure you have heard of the unfortunate tragedy that has befallen the nation of St. Michel?"

What? What does this have to do with the situation? Sophie nodded guardedly. Who didn't know about it? The accident had commanded the headlines for the past three days. Her mother was a huge fan of the St. Michel royal family and had called, in tears, the moment she'd heard about it. For as far back as Sophie could remember, Rose had kept a scrapbook on the House of Founteneau. But that wasn't the reason the tragedy had touched Sophie so deeply.

It was kind of silly…but she felt bad for the king of St. Michel. It was crazy and almost a little celebrity obsessive, and she wasn't infatuated with the St. Michel royals—she just knew about them by virtue of her mother's fixation. Still, that a father should outlive all his children was more than any parent should bear. Savannah was her life. She couldn't bear to think of losing her.

Sophie whispered a silent prayer for the king—one parent to another.

"Because of the sad turn of events, I have come to seek your assistance," said Luc

Assistance?

Virtual warning lights flashed in Sophie's head. *Wait a minute, buster.* She glanced at her parents for some indication of what this was about, but neither would make eye contact.

"How on earth could I help you with anything having to do with St. Michel?"

"It's a very complicated story," Luc said. "But you are the only one who can help King Bertrand. Would you care to sit down while I explain?" He looked her square in the eyes and flashed that smile of his—a smile that could probably talk the pants off any woman…or talk all the money right out of someone's bank account. But Luc Lejardin had no idea whom he was dealing with. She was on to him and his rat scheme.

Weren't tricks like this mostly confined to e-mails where the scammer, safely cloaked in the anonymity of cyberspace, *humbly begs your pardon, but has chosen you out of all the people in the world to help transfer millions of dollars out of a fictitious Ivory Coast bank?*

"So con artists are making house calls?" she said.

Luc looked confused. *Oh,* he was cute *and* he was a good actor. The guy had skills. Yeah, and using the Founteneau tragedy to scam others—and her mother would be the perfect target—was lower than low.

"Get out now. All of you." Sophie pointed toward the door. "Or I'll call the police."

"Oh, Sophie, no," said Rose.

"I don't mean you, Mom. You and Dad stay right there. I want *them* out. Now."

She pulled out her cell phone and started punching in 911.

"No, don't. Please." Luc held up his hands in surrender. "I know this sounds incredible, but please hear me out. Please allow me to explain."

"Sophie, hear him out," her father demanded.

Dear God, did Luc have her father snowed, too? Still, there was something in her dad's expression that preempted Sophie from completing the call.

For one very short moment.

Holding her finger over the dial button, she said, "Mr. Lejardin, you have exactly ten seconds to explain. Starting now."

He nodded.

"Your Highness, forgive me for speaking so plainly, but you are the granddaughter of King Bertrand. He requests that you come to St. Michel so that he might talk to you about assuming your rightful place as heiress to the throne of St. Michel."

Your Highness? For a moment, Sophie's knees threatened to buckle, but then a wave of anger so strong she thought she'd breathed fire coursed through her. To keep from scream-ing at the ridiculous man, she controlled her voice, letting the rage bleed through loud and clear.

"What kind of fool do you take me for? What do you want? Money? Well, I don't have any. Neither do my parents. And you'd better stay the hell away from my daughter because if you lay one finger on her, I will rip you apart with my bare hands—"

All of a sudden her father's arms were around her. "*Mon Dieu,* my love," he soothed. "*Shh.* Don't talk like that."

Only then did Sophie realize that she'd been shouting.

"Listen to me," John pleaded, looking down at her as tears misted his eyes. "Come. Sit. Listen to what we have to say."

Sophie looked from him to her mother trying to make sense out of the absurd assertions.

"It's true," Rose said, bowing her head. "Monsieur Lejardin speaks the truth."

Sophie glanced back at Luc, hoping beyond hope that he wouldn't be there. If he disappeared, that would mean this was one of those bizarre dreams where you wake up and laugh about how ridiculous it was— *Ha ha! Imagine that. Me, the princess of St. Michel. What a hoot.*

But Luc Lejardin was there. Handsome as ever. Standing in her living room, gazing at her with those eyes and looking way too polished and sophisticated amidst her shabby chic furnishings.

She allowed her father to lead her to the couch.

As she settled between her parents, Luc motioned for his men to leave the room.

"Mom? What's going on?" Savannah's voice cut through the surreal haze. The girl stood in the hall that led to the bedrooms. Emo Jess's tattooed boyfriend was with her, looking pale and dangerous with his spiky black hair and pierced bottom lip.

Sophie didn't quite know how to answer her daughter's question. She certainly didn't want to get into it in front of Flea—or Tick—she couldn't remember his name without the benefit of reading the tattoo on Jess's neck.

In fact, as motherly concern vied with the confusion over the royal revelation, she wanted to ask her daughter the same question.

What is going on, Savannah? Why is that boy here?

But she couldn't form the words. Even so, she could do the math in her head: Emo Jess was absent. Her daughter looked rumpled and pink-cheeked and totally wrong with Emo Jess's boyfriend's arm slung casually around her shoulder, his limp hand dangling dangerously close to her daughter's right breast.

That's what her mother meant about having a boy over.... Had they skipped school and been here alone in this house all morning?

Oh, dear God.

Had the whole world turned inside out? Because everything seemed to be upside down today and sliding toward a big black hole that used to be the center of their lives.

Somehow, miraculously, Sophie found her voice.

"We're having a family meeting, Savannah. Your friend needs to leave."

The boy didn't say a word, but he remained, looking scuzzy in his low-slung, skinny jeans and ripped black T-shirt.

Expressionless. And still *touching* her daughter.

Savannah reached up and took his hand. "Tick doesn't

want to leave. If this has something to do with me, he can stay. We have no secrets from each other."

Rose gasped.

"No, he needs to leave," Sophie insisted.

The boy still didn't budge.

At a loss, Sophie glanced from her daughter to her parents, to Luc, whose piercing dark gaze snared and held hers.

The next thing she knew, Luc was hulking over the kid. Then, without touching him, he was showing Tick the door.

"Oh my *Gaaaawd*," Savannah whined. "I cannot believe he just did that. How could you let him do that to me, Mom?"

It was all too much.

Too. Much.

All crashing down on her at once.

"Go to your room. We'll talk about this later."

Savannah stomped off.

A door slammed.

Sophie bristled.

"Are you going to let her get away with talking to you like that?" Rose asked.

Sophie turned to her mother. "I don't let her *get away with* anything. However, right now, I think I have another situation I need to deal with first."

Her mother seemed to shrink back in her seat.

Luc was in her line of vision, wearing an expression that ranged somewhere between disbelief and disgust. She wanted to say, "Well, Mr. Armani Suit, you've obviously never lived with a teenager. Try it sometime, then we'll talk."

She could feel her left eyelid twitch as she forced a smile. "So, where were we?"

The four of them sat in silence until finally her mother

cleared her throat and spoke. "Many years ago your father and I worked for King Bertrand of St. Michel. In order to avoid a scandal that would have potentially destroyed the House of Founteneau, he sent his daughter into top-secret confinement before anyone even knew the girl was pregnant. Then when the child was born, he secretly adopted her out. Princesse Sylvie was only seventeen years old, after all. She thought she was madly in love with that rock star Nick Morrison. You've probably heard of him. The king would have no part of it and did what he thought was best for his daughter and his country."

Sophie shuddered inwardly as she thought of Savannah coming to the same pregnant fate after spending the day alone with that boy.

"Don't you understand where this is leading?" Rose beseeched.

Sophie blinked at her mother. Feeling as if she'd missed something, she shook her head. "Oh, this just keeps getting better and better. I can't imagine where it's going."

Rose silenced her with a wave.

Sophie shrugged and traced the floral pattern on the sofa cushion with her finger.

"Sweetheart, *we* were the couple who adopted the *princesse's* baby. We named her Sophie and raised her and loved her as our own. *You* were that baby."

As her mother's words became clear, the edges of Sophie's vision closed in. She heard her father's voice now, as if it were streaming through a long tunnel.

"We never told you because we pledged secrecy to the king," he said, as if that were supposed to make everything all right. "We were his humble servants. We were honored he would entrust his granddaughter to us and felt duty-bound to keep our word."

Sophie stood up fast—too fast—and Luc caught her by the elbow as she wavered. His touch was sure and strong, and she was positive he could see right through her to her shaky, scared inner child. A child who'd been suddenly stripped of the only life she'd ever known, orphaned by the revelation of a well-guarded secret.

"Excuse me." She pulled away and walked over to the window, needing space, needing to see something familiar to help her make sense of this bombshell.

The first things she saw were the three *Men in Black* sitting on her porch in the freezing cold…which reinforced the fact that her parents weren't her parents. She was the daughter of a dead princess and a rock legend whose CDs were in her collection.

It was incomprehensible. Totally and completely absurd. Like some sort of bad joke—

Wait a minute.

She whirled around. "This is a *joke,* right? Like *Candid Camera* or *Punked?* Well, if it is, it's not funny. In fact, it's really pathetic given what's happened in St. Michel."

Nobody said a word. They didn't have to. Their grave faces told her everything she needed to know.

"Oh, my good God." Her voice trembled and seemed to come from somewhere outside her body. "I have to get out of here."

It was Luc's job to stay one step ahead of the situation. He was good at reading people and circumstances. As Sophie grabbed her purse and keys, Luc anticipated her next move and headed her off at the front door.

"Get out of my way." Her green eyes blazed and threatened that she might hit him if he didn't move. It wouldn't be the first time a woman's hand had smarted his face.

"*Pardonnez-moi,* Your Highness, but I cannot allow you to go out unattended."

Her pale cheeks flushed, and she stubbornly tilted her chin.

"You've got to be kidding me. You can't hold me prisoner in my own house."

Strange, though, he hadn't expected the protective empathy he'd feel for her. Usually, he had no problem compartmentalizing his feelings—a must for someone in his position—so that he could keep a clear head and get a proper read on situations as they presented themselves.

For some reason, perhaps because of Antoine, this case felt different. Hit a tad too close to home.

"Your Highness—"

"Stop calling me that."

"Very well then, *Madame,* given what just happened to the prince—your uncle," Luc bowed his head out of respect, "I cannot allow you to leave alone."

"It's Sophie."

"I beg your pardon, *Madame?*"

"Stop with the *Your Highness* and *Madame.* My name is Sophie, and I'd appreciate it if you stick to that."

The photos didn't do her justice. Her eyes were nearly the shade of emeralds. Paired with her dark hair they really made a striking contrast.

"If you insist, *Sophie.*" It felt improper—too intimate—to call her by her given name. "I have no intention of holding you prisoner. If you would like to leave, there is a car outside and I would be happy to escort you anywhere you would care to go."

"So you're saying if I walk out of this house, you'll follow me?"

Luc nodded.

Following her would not be so unpalatable.

He blinked away the inappropriate thought and focused on the reality of the situation: As a servant of the royal family he couldn't *force* her to do anything against her will. He could only make strong suggestions and, if all else failed, he'd resort to charm.

Whatever it took. Because he had less than twenty-four hours to convince her to come back to St. Michel, or they'd be forced to switch to Plan B, which involved King Bertrand coming to Trevard to close the deal himself.

Luc really didn't want it to come to that.

"What if I call the police?" Sophie threatened.

"I cannot stop you from doing so, but I ask you to consider the consequences. If you involve the authorities, the media will most likely get wind of this. Once the story breaks, the security threat for you and your family will increase one hundredfold. You won't even be able to get out of your front door because media from all over the world will be camping on your lawn."

Sophie's eyes widened, looking pure and green and innocent. Clearly she hadn't considered this possibility.

"If you won't think of your own safety," Rose called from the living room, "consider Savannah's."

"I'm not talking to you and Dad right now," Sophie answered back, then immediately squeezed her eyes shut as if she regretted her words.

Neither Rose nor John responded. Gauging Sophie's expression, Luc couldn't tell if that made things better or worse.

She sighed.

"Come on," she said, her voice a hissed whisper. "You and I are going somewhere private where we can talk. I want the whole story and I want you to give it to me straight."

After Luc instructed his men to keep close watch on the place, Sophie softened her tone and asked her parents to tell Savannah she'd be back before bedtime.

Two minutes later, she and Luc were in the back of his rented Lincoln Town Car, heading toward the highway.

"Where would you like to go?" the driver asked.

She shrugged. "Just drive for a while. I need to get away from here so I can think."

They rode in silence for about forty-five minutes. Sophie sat next to Luc staring out of the passenger window. Luc could see her profile in three-quarter view.

She looked like Princesse Sylvie, he thought. The spitting image of her, or what he imagined she would've looked like had she lived. Those who died young were forever immortalized in perpetual youth. Never aging, the patina of youth growing more beautiful with each passing year.

"Has anyone ever told you how much you look like your mother?"

"Which one?" she asked, with a sardonic quirk of her brow.

"Princesse Sylvie, of course."

Sophie laughed, though there wasn't much humor in the dry sound. "The funny thing is people used to tell me all the time how much Rose and I looked alike…. I never saw it. Now I know why."

"It is a bit unnerving how much you resembled the late *princesse*. A tad—" Luc searched for the right word "—*stupéfiant.*"

"Stupefying, huh?" The right side of her mouth twitched, but the humor gave way to a softer expression. "What was she like?"

Now they were getting somewhere.

"She had quite a zest for life. *La joie* is how we call it. That love of life seemed to radiate from her every pore. She gave your grandfather quite a challenge, though. The press loved to photograph her—dancing the nights away in Paris and sunbathing on the deck of some baron's yacht on the Côte d'Azur. Always with that devil-may-care gleam in her eyes. You have her eyes, you know? Many thought of her as the ideal woman. Yet, those who knew her best said she was a very kind person."

Sophie didn't look impressed.

"Did you have crush on Princesse Sylvie, Monsieur Lejardin?"

He flinched. "I beg your pardon?"

Sophie laughed. "A *crush,* you know, to be intrigued with, to have the hots for. A crush."

She was toying with him. Even so, it was good to see her lighten up a bit.

"I have always held the late *princesse* in the highest esteem."

"Well, I would expect nothing less from you," she conceded as they approached a quaint restaurant fashioned to look like a log cabin. "Stop here, please. I need some coffee."

Luc assessed the place as the driver steered the car off the road into the gravel driveway. It looked harmless enough, out here in the middle of nowhere. Two cars dotted the parking lot. Not busy. If they had to stop, this was probably as good a place as any.

When they walked in, he was relieved to see that indeed the place was nearly empty, except for a flannel-clad couple sitting on red and silver swivel stools at the Formica counter, having pie and coffee.

He'd never seen anything like this place. It was a regular Norman Rockwell depiction of middle America. Like a quaint foreign country he was visiting for the first time.

"Y'all grab a seat anywhere ya like," the waitress drawled from behind the counter.

They settled into a back-corner booth.

He picked up a menu—mostly out of curiosity, to see what type of food one found in a place like this. Standard American fare: burgers, French fries, milk shakes. Some of the items he wasn't familiar with: grits? hash browns? red-eye gravy?

After the waitress served the coffee—if you could call the thin, caramel-colored water she poured into the cups coffee—Sophie asked wearily, "So, what happens next?"

Luc stirred a packet of sugar into the hot liquid.

"I would like to take you and your daughter back to St. Michel to meet King Bertrand."

She looked at him as if he'd suggested she re-create Sylvie's nude sunbathing escapades.

Again, he found himself blinking away the image of her lounging, cat-like on the bow of an expensive cigarette boat.

"I don't think so," she said.

"Why not?" he asked. "Aren't you at all curious about your country?"

"You just don't get it, do you?"

He shrugged.

"I suppose not. Would you care to explain?"

She put her palms flat on the table and leaned toward him.

"I have two jobs. Savannah has school. We can't just drop everything because King Grandpa beckons."

King Grandpa? For some reason, the phrase struck him as funny and he had to purse his lips to keep from smiling because this was not a time to make light.

Except that the more he talked to Sophie, the more she proved to be like her mother. Strong-willed, irreverent… smart, funny.

He dragged a hand over his jaw in an effort to control the deluge of awareness that coursed through him. An awareness the likes of which he hadn't felt in a very long time.

Why her? Well, that was easy enough to answer. She was *magnifique*. But why did she have to be the king's granddaughter?

That made the situation hopeless.

His family name had nearly come to ruin because of indiscretion and it had taken all he and his two brothers had to rebuild it. He would not lose everything they had worked so hard to reconstruct by developing a schoolboy crush on the king's granddaughter.

He took a long, slow sip of coffee and mentally packaged up the remnants of those thoughts, tucking them away where they would be a nonissue.

He shrugged. "If you refuse to go, King Bertrand will simply come to you."

She looked exasperated.

"I'm not ready to talk to him. He has to understand that this has all come out of left field. I haven't had a chance to digest it yet."

Luc sipped his coffee again, buying himself time. It wasn't his place to offer advice to Sophie. However, it was his job to ensure she would listen and ultimately agree to what the king proposed.

"If I may be so bold as to offer you something to consider." He returned his cup to the saucer. "As Princesse Sylvie's illegitimate daughter, you would've lived a life wracked with scandal. You would've paid for your mother's mistake."

Her jaw dropped and her right brow arched.

"So that's all I am to the king? A mistake?"

"Don't twist my words. Even though it might not appear so on the surface, the king did the right thing by sending you away. He gave you a better life."

She grimaced. "Right. While Gramps lived the high life in his ivory tower, I've been working two jobs to put food on the table for my daughter. Yeah, that's a much better life than he's lived, I'm sure."

"You've only struggled since your divorce last year."

She set her cup down hard and coffee sloshed over the rim. "How do you know this? It freaks me out more than just a little that you know so much about me. Especially given that until a few hours ago I had no idea you even existed. You know about my divorce; how to contact my parents; where I live; where I work, I'm sure. Is that right? Do you know that?"

He wanted to tell her that he even knew what kind of underwear she'd recently purchased—the value five-pack of white Hanes cotton briefs, and that he thought she deserved more than that—but thought better of it. "It's my job to know these things."

She curled her lip. "Do you have any idea how sickening it feels to know that your life is an open book that everyone but you has read?"

Luc considered this for a moment. Yes, he did. If not the world, at least all of St. Michel. He knew how it felt to watch the intimate details that ruined his father play out in a very public arena. He'd watched his stepmother's improprieties take such a toll on his father that they eventually took his life.

At least Sophie's divorce had been private. However, that did not diminish the hurt she obviously suffered at the indiscretions of her ex-husband.

And what kind of a moron would let this woman go?

The empathy that had clouded his judgment threatened again, and he knew he'd better steer back to solid ground.

"You have been struggling since your divorce. That's a very real concern, but financial woes can be a thing of the past if you take your rightful place as the heiress to the throne of St. Michel. You'll never have to worry about money again."

Sophie bristled.

"I don't want the king's money. I'm simply making a point that my grandfather didn't do me any favors by shipping me off. Let's not pretend it was a noble deed."

Luc stifled a sigh. Yes, she absolutely had the tenacity of the late *princesse*. And it was just that dogged stubbornness that would make her a good candidate to succeed her grandfather.

"It was a difficult decision for your grandfather to make. It wasn't easy for John and Rose to keep the secret all these years, but they did so not only out of duty, but also out of compassion. They did it out of love for you. Couldn't you at least hear what the king has to say?"

"Excuse me? I'm not going to drop everything and jump just because King Bertrand snaps his royal fingers. If life as

Princess Sylvie's mistake would've been so hard to endure back then, what's going to make it any different now?"

"Times have changed. People are more open-minded. Plus, you would be welcomed with open arms because…." He couldn't bring himself to say it out loud…that all of the Founteneau heirs were…dead. "Let's just say you'd be welcomed with open arms by a country that loves its royal family."

Sophie squeezed her eyes shut and leaned her head back against the booth wall, as if trying to block him out. From that angle, her lips looked soft and sensual. Luc felt another surprising stir of desire.

He gave himself a mental shake. His job was to ensure the safety of Princesse Sophie and her family, not contemplate the taste of her lips.

Merde. This was no time to blur the lines of…protocol.

He'd been immersed in work since rising to the post of minister of protocol three years ago. In his position, with his proximity to the king, he had to be careful, especially when it came to matters of the heart. He'd witnessed firsthand the fallout from getting involved with the wrong person. That's why it had been so long since he'd been serious about a woman.

She opened her eyes and said, "If the king wants to talk to me he'll have to come here. I don't have time to jet off to Europe right now."

Luc nodded. "I will let him know and he will probably arrive tomorrow."

When they arrived at Sophie's home, Rose and John were asleep, fully dressed, in the recliners in the living room. The TV was turned to half-mute, playing an infomercial for a food chopper.

Luc walked Sophie inside and started the interior perimeter check, ensuring everything was locked and secure.

But he wasn't prepared for the shattering sound of Sophie Baldwin's scream.

Chapter Three

When Sophie opened the door to Savannah's dark bedroom to kiss her good-night, the last thing she expected to see was a figure launch itself off her daughter's bed, in one swift cat-like motion.

That image, and the echoes of Luc's security warnings, elicited a scream so loud it could've woken up the whole of western North Carolina.

She flipped on the lights. Tick stood there. Although they were both fully clothed, Savannah groped to pull her shirt into place. Sophie's fear morphed into mother-tiger–like rage.

"What the hell do you think you're doing?" she demanded.

By that time Luc's men were in the room and they had Tick's left arm yanked so far behind his back it was a wonder she didn't hear the pop of his shoulder dislocating.

"Get him out of here," Luc ordered.

"Don't hurt him!" Savannah jumped from the bed and started beating on the security agent who had Tick pinned.

Before Sophie could pull Savannah away, the guys had Tick out of the room. Luc strategically headed off Savannah so she couldn't follow. Sophie watched the scene unfold as if in slow motion, feeling more than ever as if her life was totally beyond her control.

"Let me go!" Savannah screamed. "You can't do this to us!"

"Savannah, you are fourteen years old," Sophie said. "You have no business allowing a boy in your room, much less in your bed."

The girl quit struggling.

"I love him and he loves me. He told me so."

Oh, baby, you don't know what love is. Even though you think you do, it won't last. It never does.

But she knew better than to spew her jaded views of the heart on her daughter. She had to focus on what was important. The boy had been in Savannah's bed. Even if her daughter had no intention of having sex, she put herself in a very bad position.

"Of course he's going to tell you he loves you." She softened her voice. "He might really mean it, although it's hard to believe since just last week he was slobbering all over Jess."

Savannah rolled her eyes.

"What would you know about love? You couldn't even stay married to Daddy."

Sophie flinched. If Savannah was looking for the best poison arrow to shoot, that was the one.

It pierced Sophie right through the heart.

She must not have been able to disguise the pain because Luc grimaced and gave her a sign over the girl's head that said *I'll leave you two alone.* He slipped out of the room, leaving her to face her daughter on her own.

Savannah didn't seem to notice his exit—or maybe she was ignoring it. She walked back over to her bed and flopped down.

Sophie stared at her, wondering what had happened to her daughter who was once so sweet. The obvious answer was this creature who called himself Tick, but Sophie couldn't follow that thought through. Besides, this change had been coming on slowly since Frank left. Maybe Sophie had been too soft on her. If so, it was born of good intentions. She thought she was doing the right thing, protecting her daughter, letting the moodiness and flippant quips slide, being her daughter's punching bag to soften the blow this divorce had had on Savannah.

It hit her all at once that rather than helping her daughter, she'd created a monster.

"I know things have been hard since your dad left, but that doesn't give you a license to be disrespectful." Her voice was soft but firm. "You've been disrespectful to me a lot lately and I'm tired of it. As much as I hate to have to do this, I'm going to have to ground you for that and for skipping school and having that boy in your room."

"How could your men let him in?" Standing in the living room, Sophie glared at Luc with burning reproachful eyes.

It was true. While he and the *princesse* were out, the boy simply knocked on the door, asked to see Savannah, and was allowed to enter.

Tick hadn't been identified as a security threat or otherwise been named as a person who should be barred. So when the boy followed the proper procedure for admittance—that is, knocking on the front door—the agent let him in.

This explanation didn't do a thing to appease Sophie.

"Common sense should scream that you don't leave a teenage boy and girl alone in a bedroom." She sputtered with indignation. "Come on, you were a teenager once. Think about it."

She had a point.

Still, if there was one thing Luc didn't understand, it was teenage girls. Princesse Sophie had her hands full with that one.

Luc was in a precarious position. While he was responsible for the young *princesse,* he and his men weren't at liberty to correct her behavior without express orders from the royal family.

"And Mom, where were you and Dad?"

At least she was still calling Rose and John Mom and Dad.

The older woman shrugged and stared at her hands. "We were in the kitchen. We didn't even hear him arrive.

"Sophie, I know you're upset with us right now and what I'm about to suggest will possibly aggravate the situation, but this behavior isn't like Savannah. Do you suppose it's her way of crying for help? I know she's been upset since her dad left and you've been out of the house more working. Even though it's unfortunate what happened to Prince Antoine, God rest his soul," Rose looked up to the heavens and crossed herself, "going to St. Michel might be an opportunity for you to reconnect with your daughter."

John nodded. "Take that girl to St. Michel. Get her away

from here, from all this confusion and that boy who seems to have cast such a spell on her."

Sophie gaped at her parents as if they spoke a foreign language.

"I just don't know if moving is the best thing for my daughter."

The first fingers of early morning light reached through the blinds and shook Sophie awake. She'd spent a restless night tossing and turning. Now it was time to get up and face another day. Yesterday seemed like a strange dream and what lay in store for today seemed so big it was almost overwhelming.

Especially the parts that involved Savannah.

Sophie hated to go to bed when she and Savannah were mad at each other, but last night she knew it was for the best that they let their emotions cool. She wasn't so much mad at her daughter as she was disappointed.

There was a time not so long ago when Sophie's being disappointed in her would've mattered to Savannah; when disappointment would've been worse than any punishment Sophie could've dished out. Then again, that was when Savannah loved Elmo and thought boys were yucky.

It was okay that boys weren't the enemy anymore—especially in light of the divorce. But finding a boy in Savannah's bedroom—Sophie shuddered and sat up and hugged her knees.

Straight off this morning, not only did she have to discuss boys with her daughter, she also had to break the news—*Oh, by the way, you're a princess and the great-grandfather you never knew—who also happens to be the king of St. Michel is stopping by for a visit this afternoon.*

The thought made her flop back down onto the bed, as if

the enormity of the situation physically weighed her down. Was going back to bed and pulling the covers over her head an option today?

It wasn't.

She had to get up and face this day head-on.

Even though yesterday Savannah had been too self-absorbed to be concerned about anything that was happening outside the orbit of her teenage world, she was bound to ask why the *Men in Black* were still hanging around today.

Sophie wasn't sure how Savannah would react to the news. Because she wasn't quite sure she even knew her daughter these days.

She partially blamed herself for this change in Savannah's behavior—for not being around enough. But darn it, she was doing the best she could.

The only thing that was certain was that she wouldn't get anything done lying in bed. She sat up, put her feet on the floor and prepared for battle.

It was already nine o'clock, but Sophie decided to shower and dress before waking Savannah. And a half-hour later she stood outside her daughter's room in her bathrobe with her hair in a towel and no idea what she was going to say. She took a deep breath. Muffled voices and cooking sounds came from the direction of the kitchen, along with the smell of coffee. She could certainly do with a good strong cup before she met Savannah head-on, but she needed to talk to her daughter alone without her parents listening in and mostly without the distraction of Luc Lejardin.

She let herself into Savannah's dark room, opened the blind so that soft light filtered into the room and sat down on the edge of her daughter's bed.

"Savannah, honey, wake up. We need to talk."

* * *

Part one of Sophie's heart-to-heart with Savannah went surprisingly well. It started off a little rocky with plenty of pleas such as "Mom, you've just got to give Tick a chance" and "We're in love."

Still, as Sophie held her ground, eventually Savannah softened and even ended up apologizing and admitted that letting the boy into her room was a mistake. Sitting there on the bed next to each other, they talked a little about how their relationship had changed since the divorce. Savannah opened up and acknowledged that she knew she shouldn't blame her mother.

"Dad was the one who left." She stared at her hands for a moment, then with tears in her eyes, she reached out and hugged Sophie and said, "I love you so much, Mom. I'm sorry I've been treating you so bad. I don't know why I do it."

"Maybe because it feels safe to be mad at me?" She whispered into her daughter's ear.

Because you know I'll always be here.

She thought about Rose and wondered if that wasn't exactly why she felt free enough to be so angry at her own mother?

A mother who wasn't really her mother.

A mother who'd kept this secret of who they really were tucked away all these years.

Panic blossomed in her chest, and Sophie hugged Savannah tighter to block out the hurt and confusion. Instead she concentrated on keeping her relationship with her own daughter on track.

Ugh, she hated to spoil it with the *princess revelation*, but she had no choice. According to Luc, the king was due to arrive that afternoon and it would be far worse if Savannah were blindsided by his appearance.

It was almost as if fate was in her corner, because as Sophie was weighing her words, figuring out how to broach the subject, Savannah pulled out of the embrace and said, "So are you ever going to tell me why those men were here with Grandma and Grandpa yesterday?"

Sophie forced a smile. "Well, I thought you'd never ask."

Her voice sounded a little too bright, as if she were going to follow it up with, *They're here to escort us to Disney World, for a private, behind-the-scenes tour.*

Obviously Savannah caught the false note. She furrowed her brow and said, "Okay, what gives, Mom?"

Luc paced the length of the living room, feeling like a caged animal—or worse yet, a man with a job to do held hostage by an ambivalent *princesse.*

He still didn't know whether Sophie would agree to the king's proposal. He should've clinched that deal yesterday. That was his job, after all.

Everything hinged on Savannah.

He and Sophie had agreed that she would break the news to her daughter. But he didn't understand why, against his advisement, she'd waited until the very last minute to do so.

Sure there was the unfortunate incident of discovering that boy in the girl's room last night, but he didn't understand why Sophie didn't just take charge of the girl and lay down the law. Tell her how things would be and be done with it.

Lord knew the woman was stubborn enough. He couldn't figure out why she didn't make this easier on everyone and use some of that will on her daughter.

In his mind's eye he could see her lifting her lovely chin and meeting his gaze with an icy, defiant stare. Much to his dismay, he found that strength appealing—in an exasperating, irksome way he didn't quite understand. Or maybe it was more apt to say it irked him because he didn't want to find anything about Sophie Baldwin appealing.

Restless and irritable, Luc sat on the chintz sofa and went over the morning's plan one more time: He was due to leave within the hour to make sure the airfield was secure for King Bertrand's arrival late that afternoon. This was a particularly challenging task because he had to ensure the usual level of security for the king, while at the same time not drawing any unnecessary attention to them.

It would be disastrous if word got out prematurely, as they hadn't yet advised the St. Michel Crown Council of Sophie's existence.

As much as he hated to work clandestinely, there were too many variables, namely Sophie and Savannah's safety and whether Sophie would cooperate.

Much to Luc's dismay, her cooperation remained the number one variable. Was he losing his touch? When it came to matters of state security, he never had a problem getting the job done. Especially when it involved members of the opposite sex.

But *princesse* or not, Sophie was not typical. As experience had taught him, most women would trade their soul for the chance to don a title and the crown jewels. His stepmother was an embarrassing case in point. She'd all but ruined the Lejardin name in her quest to get ahead.

All of this and more was being handed to Sophie on a royal cushion. Yet she wasn't sure she wanted any part of it.

That's what made her so maddeningly interesting—and Luc's job so much harder.

If she refused, it was best to keep her blood ties to the royal family quiet.

To that end, they'd taken all possible precautions to prevent the media from getting wind of King Bertrand's trip to Trevard—the king and his entourage would fly into Washington, D.C., ostensibly to visit the St. Michel Embassy. Then he and a pared-down staff consisting of his personal secretary and three security agents would fly in, landing at a rural airstrip just outside of Trevard. Luc would meet them there and escort them to Sophie's house.

The flight crew was on the king's payroll, and the king's personal secretary, Marci, understood the delicate nature of the king's business—even if she didn't know the details. So there was no worry about the press getting wind of the king's arrival. Luc would be there to ensure that everything went according to plan.

He checked his watch.

Sophie and Savannah still hadn't emerged from their bedchambers. It was enough to make him get up and start pacing again.

"I just brewed a fresh pot of coffee, Luc," Rose called from the kitchen. "Why don't you come in and pour yourself a cup?"

Rose kept insisting that everything would be fine, that Sophie would cooperate. But she hardly seemed clearheaded about it. One moment she was busily cooking and bustling about readying the place for the king. The next minute she was fretting over Sophie, about how she never dreamed things would turn out this way; then in the next breath, she was encouraging Luc to have faith that Sophie would do the right thing, that he should just give her some space.

He wondered if the pep talk wasn't as much for Rose's own benefit, because she was obviously worried about the damage that had been done to their mother–daughter relationship.

He poured himself a cup of coffee and sat at the small, round kitchen table, which was covered with fresh brioche and other confections that Rose had been baking for the king.

"King Bertrand always was crazy about my brioche," she said with pride. "He always told me that none could top mine. And of course there's no place in Trevard to purchase it. So I thought I'd make some for him."

"I'm sure he will be deeply appreciative." He sipped his coffee. "She doesn't strike me as the type to hold a grudge."

Rose looked a little startled as she glanced over the top of her wire-rimmed glasses. She was pouring chocolate cake batter into round pans, and scraped the sides of the mixing bowl a little faster.

"*Non,* she usually doesn't," she said. "Probably because usually we don't fight. We've always had a close, loving relationship. Maybe that's why this feels like the end of the world to me."

Luc sipped his coffee. "Just like you said, give her time and she'll come around. She'll realize that a parent is more than just a flesh and blood relation."

Rose put down the mixing bowl and wiped her hands on a dish towel. "You're a good man, Luc. I know in my heart Sophie will do the right thing. When she does, I will count on you to keep my girls safe."

Luc nodded as he walked to the sink to rinse his cup.

"That's my mission."

"And there's no doubt you do it well. It's just that she and Savannah are everything to John and me. You know I am loyal to King Bertrand and St. Michel, but the girls are our life."

"Then I give you my pledge I will guard them with my life."

He set his cup in the sink and went to find Sophie himself.

He felt like a trespasser in the hall that led to the bedrooms and even worse when he strained to listen to what the female voices coming from the last door on the left were saying. As he made his way toward the voices, he glanced inside an open door.

Sophie's room.

It was unfamiliar and grippingly female territory.

Feeling like a voyeur, he drank in every detail of her private quarters: the unmade bed in which *she* slept; the rumpled white sheets twisted amidst the powder-blue eyelet duvet cover; her nightgown draped across the foot of the bed. The scent of her hung in the air—floral and spice and something maddeningly feminine.

Tension tightened in his belly as he fought a sudden urge to step inside the room and press the silky nightdress to his face and savor the essence of her.

But the murmur of conversation from the room down the hall rose in pitch, then fell back into the same indecipherable hum, and he blinked away irrational thoughts of that gown and nothing else on Sophie's naked skin.

He turned away from the room and made his way down the hall and knocked. The voices stopped for a moment before Sophie opened the door.

Her wet hair softly framed her face. She looked freshly scrubbed, standing there barefoot in a soft pink terry robe that revealed just a hint of cleavage that kept tempting his eyes to fall.

"Good morning." Luc looked her squarely in the eyes.

The look on Sophie's face was anything but welcoming. "Good morning. Don't tell me *he's* here already."

Behind Sophie, Savannah glared at him from the bed where she sat clutching a pillow. The mood barometer registered dangerous thunderstorms.

"No, King Bertrand has not arrived as of yet. He'll be here late this afternoon. But I will be leaving in a few moments to take care of some matters before he comes, and I wanted to brief you and your daughter before I left."

From the look on Sophie's face, you would've thought he'd asked her go and pick up King Bertrand herself.

"I'm sort of in the middle of something here."

Sophie glanced back at her daughter, then stepped into the hall, brushing against Luc as she closed the door behind her. They stood so close, he recognized hints of the same intoxicating scent he'd smelled in her bedroom. To his relief, she gathered the lapel of her robe and held it closed.

"I was telling her about the situation and she's a little confused," Sophie whispered. "She's just started high school and she thinks she's in love—although I'd move to St. Michel just to get her away from that boy."

Was it her shampoo or perfume…?

Whatever it was, it tempted him to lean in closer.

"Plus she has this crazy notion that her father and I will get back together again someday. She thinks if we leave, that won't happen."

This suggestion caught him off guard and instantly sobered him.

"If you stay will it happen?"

Sophie blinked at him.

"Of course not."

He found himself exhaling a breath he hadn't realized he'd been holding. At least she didn't seem to be pining over her ex-husband. Thank God. A woman like Sophie deserved better than the jerk he had read about in her file. "Look, I think it's best if you brief me and let me relay any instructions to my daughter. Like me, she needs a little time to digest the situation."

The briefing. Right. The job he'd come to do. He was irritated with himself for getting sidetracked in such a foolish way.

He glanced at his watch. "I hope she will be able to—how do you say—*digest* the situation soon, because the king will expect her cooperation as well as yours."

Sophie glared at him.

She looked weary and fragile and beautiful. He felt guilty for continuing to press the matter.

"I understand that he is the king of St. Michel," she said. "But in my house he's a guest. *An uninvited guest.* So don't climb up on your high horse and expect me to fall on my knees. If my daughter isn't ready to meet him when he gets here, he'll have to accept it. I'm not even sure *I* want to meet him."

Chapter Four

When King Bertrand arrived at Sophie's house at 5:30, Rose and John fell to their knees in reverence.

Even Sophie, who'd vowed to hold tight to her you-put-your-pants-on-one-leg-at-a-time-just-like-the-rest-of-us resolve, was a little taken aback by the sight of him. It was weird seeing the king of St. Michel in his fine suit, a little grayer and a bit smaller than he looked in the media; so out of context standing in the middle of her living room.

Out of the corner of her eye, she caught a glimpse of her mother, who was still on her knees, glaring at her. Sophie glared back. Rose redoubled her glower and motioned toward the ground with her head, obviously insisting that Sophie should join her in this show of subservience.

But by that time, King Bertrand, who appeared oblivious to Sophie's lapse of etiquette—actually, he seemed to not even notice Sophie at all—said, "Please rise. Rose, John, it's been far too long."

He hugged the couple one at a time, greeting them like old friends he was genuinely happy to see.

Tears streamed down her mother's face, and she couldn't recall another time when her father stood so tall and beamed with such pride.

She felt a little bad for being so mutinous.

"You have served St. Michel well," said the king, "and you will be duly rewarded once we return."

Hmm…once who returns?

The king turned to Sophie. "The tragic loss of my son and his family is not only cause for great personal sadness, but it is also cause for concern for the entire country. Without someone with Founteneau blood running through *her* veins, the 750-year-old Founteneau dynasty will end upon my death. If that happens, a collateral heir will be chosen by St. Michel's Crown Council, the administrative body that advises me on domestic and international affairs."

"Yes, I understand what the Crown Council does," Sophie said. "Luc has been very good about filling me in."

"Yes, well…there is no way I will allow the Founteneau dynasty to fall. That's why you must immediately come back to St. Michel and accept your rightful place as heir to the throne and eventually become the queen."

Sophie nearly snorted her coffee. "*Me? A queen?* You've got to be kidding me?"

It was all she could do to make it to work on time and manage her client load. How in the world was she supposed to run an entire country?

"Don't get ahead of yourself. As of now you're only a

princesse, but yes, because of the bloodline, eventually you will be queen. That's the point of this. Don't make it any more tedious than it needs to be."

He looked her up and down appraisingly, leaving her with the impression that she didn't measure up.

She bristled.

"You come crawling out of the woodwork and expect me to welcome you with open arms after you've sat up there on your royal high horse ignoring me all these years? Do you really expect me to drop my entire life, pack up my daughter and move to St. Michel because you beckon? What happened to my being the national embarrassment? When did I suddenly become fit to be queen?"

"Granted, Madame Baldwin, you're not ideal," he said. "But you're all we have."

Sophie wasn't sure if it was the use of her married name or the king's icy, formal tone that bothered her more. Maybe it was both heaped on top of this absurd rock-and-a-hard-spot circumstance.

A bad situation she intended to put an end to once and for all.

"You know what?" Sophie set down her coffee cup and stood. "Since the good people of St. Michel aren't any the wiser about me, let's not disappoint them. Why don't we just go ahead and let me remain the family's dirty little secret?"

Rose gasped. "Sophie, you don't mean that. Your Majesty, she doesn't mean it."

The king looked stunned.

"Oh, yes, I do. It's clear he doesn't believe I'm suited for the job. So let's all forget this ever happened."

She started toward the door.

"Goodbye, Your Majesty. I'm sure under other circumstances it would've been a pleasure."

She stopped in the foyer. The once-so-majestic king looked downright panicked.

"Sophie, wait," Luc called after her. From this vantage point, she couldn't see his face but could imagine him. "This is awkward for everyone. Perhaps we should start over."

Feeling like a naughty child, Sophie avoided eye contact with the king as she shook her head. "I don't think so."

Luc stepped into the foyer. He was putting words in the king's mouth and it struck Sophie that at the moment, Luc seemed more regal than the man who held the royal title. But wasn't that always how it was? The real power always lay behind the throne. As a general rule, Sophie had never been drawn to powerful men, but there was something about Luc looking so confident and self-possessed in that dark suit that was downright sexy.

And that made her want to squirm.

"Perhaps we've underestimated you?" His sultry, unwavering gaze held hers.

Something about the way Luc was looking at her made her feel naked. Not the sensual, I'm-imagining-you-without-clothes-let's-get-it-on sort of naked—*au contraire*. It was the stripped-bare, see-right-through-you-to-the-center-of-your-very-being kind of naked.

It made her feel exposed and classless. As if this sophisticated Frenchman were humoring an insufferable hick who had no idea how to behave in the presence of royalty.

He put an arm around her and gently led her back into the living room, where the king and her parents silently waited.

After she was seated again, the king cleared his throat.

"You're not the Founteneaus'—how did you say?—dirty little secret." He pursed his lips—so very French, Sophie thought—and glanced at Luc, who picked up without missing a beat.

"Times have changed, Sophie. As I have told you, I am confident the wonderful people of St. Michel would see you as a saint and savior. However, in the 1970s in St. Michel, news of a seventeen-year-old princess getting knocked up by an unsavory rock-and-roll musician would've caused a great scandal. His Royal Majesty was just trying to save his daughter from a grave mistake."

There was that word again: mistake.

The king must have read her mind. His expression softened and she could see true contrition in his watery green eyes. Eyes that were nearly the same color as hers.

"Perhaps I was the one who made the mistake all those years ago." His voice cracked on the last word.

Again, Luc stepped in. "If the royal house spins the announcement of *the return of Princesse Sophie* just right, you could become a national heroine at a time when the people desperately need someone to love. You could make a real difference."

Everyone was quiet, apparently waiting for her to say something—anything. All she could think of was how once making a *real difference* was what mattered to her the most. That's why she'd gotten into social work. But somewhere along the way, that fight to change the world had become an uphill battle. Not that she was giving up. She wasn't, and she certainly didn't expect life to be a smooth, bump-free ride. What she hadn't counted on were the Marys of the world fighting her every step of the way, turning things that should be common-sense simple into obstacle courses that were harder and harder to navigate.

Ha! If she had a hard time circumventing Mary to get the job done, imagine what it must be like running a kingdom.

Besides, she liked her job. It was people like Laura who made Sophie know her work did make a difference.

"This is all well and good, but I'll need to think about it."

Everyone gaped at her as if they couldn't believe she'd have the audacity to *think about it.*

"What?" she said. "You can't expect me to just jump when you say so. I need some time to think about things."

For once it seemed as if King Bertrand understood better than the others. He stood and said, "Very well then. We'll be in touch tomorrow morning to see what you've decided. I'd also like to meet Savannah."

That was iffy. And there was a good possibility that she wouldn't have answers for him tomorrow, but because he was making his way to the door, she knew better than to say that and start the whole vicious debate over again.

Luc, Rose and John stood. This time, Sophie did, too. She wasn't feeling quite so defiant now. It was more like a jumbled ache that haunted her now. One minute it was insisting *there's no way.* Then the next, it was saying, *why not…?* But she could list at least ten quick reasons why not.

Luc escorted the king to the door, raising Sophie's hopes that he would leave with him. At least she'd be able to relax and try to remember what life was like before madness descended.

"I just don't see how you can refuse, lovey," Rose said as she started gathering cups and places onto a wooden tray.

I don't see how you could keep this from me my entire life. The words were on the tip of her tongue when the phone rang

"I'll get it," Sophie said, relieved at the distraction. Maybe it would be someone who would give her an excuse to take the handset into her room and shut herself in for an hour or two. If not, then she was definitely checking out for a nap of the same duration.

"Hello, Baldwin Residence," she said in her most melodic voice.

There was a pause and Sophie was just about to repeat herself when the voice on the other end of the line said, "Sophie? This is Mary Matthews."

Sophie tensed. *What now?* If she's calling to chew me out for leaving early yesterday without signing the reprimand—

"I'm calling with bad news. Your client Laura Hastings died last night."

Rose, John and Louis Dupré, one of Luc's men, took Savannah for an "outing" to give Sophie time to pull herself together. Initially, Rose didn't want to leave with her daughter so upset, but Sophie insisted, saying Savannah would be worried, too, and Rose should comfort her. Under duress, Rose finally agreed with the stipulation that Luc would keep a constant eye on her.

He fully expected Sophie to close herself up in her room, but to his surprise, she seemed to want to talk about it.

"The authorities can't tell if it was an accident or suicide." Sophie blotted her puffy eyes and stared off into the distance. "There's no note. But that morning, she put her kids on a plane to stay with her parents in California. Then last night, she crashed her car into a wall near her apartment.

"Mary thinks Laura committed suicide. I just can't imagine her taking her own life. She was doing so well. My

God, Luc, she came to see me yesterday morning, but I was so busy I didn't have time for her. Maybe I could've prevented it."

She succumbed to another bout of tears, buried her face in her hands and sobbed. Luc sat next to her on the bed and put an arm around her.

"Sophie, I don't think there was anything you could've done. Don't do this to yourself."

She didn't respond.

"Sophie, listen to me. I know how upsetting this is for you. I've never even met the woman and I find it very sad, but you can't blame yourself. That's not doing anyone any good."

She looked up at him, the color of her green eyes intensified through the tears.

"You don't understand, she came to me for help, but I was so busy that I couldn't talk to her. Now she's dead. Maybe if I'd made the time to talk to her things would've turned out differently. Maybe Mary's right. Maybe I'm not cut out for this type of work. Maybe I should do something else where I won't lead anyone else to suicide."

"I highly doubt that you led her to suicide. Did you consider that perhaps the best type of social work would be for you to save St. Michel—and the Founteneau dynasty? Don't think of it as doing a favor for the king, but consider it the ultimate act of paying forward a good deed—to the entire nation. At least consider visiting before you rule it out."

She shrugged.

"Nothing makes sense anymore," she whispered. "My parents aren't my parents. They're strangers who've kept a huge secret from me my entire life. Now my own grandfather wants me to come back because I can do something for him.

And don't forget Savannah and this...this Tick. And Laura...."

Her face crumpled and she was crying again. He felt like a heel, pushing too hard. He reached out and rubbed her back and gently swept a strand of hair off her tear-stained face.

Luc had no idea how it happened, but the next thing he knew, Sophie was in his arms, sobbing on his shoulder.

One minute she was turning toward him and the next, his right arm was around her.

He tilted his chin so that it rested on top of her head and stroked her hair in a soothing gesture. Her hair smelled like springtime and sunshine...lavender with a exquisite hint of something else that was entirely Sophie.

She smelled wonderful.

And he felt like a heel for pushing so hard. It wasn't an ideal time to bring up a visit to St. Michel. But for some reason—probably because he was intoxicated by her scent— he thought the idea of helping St. Michel would comfort her.

He found himself holding her tighter, relishing the scent of her, his heart aching for her and all that she'd been through.

As he searched for the right words to comfort her, he reminded himself that he was a pair of arms to comfort her, a shoulder on which she could lean. If he just focused on that—and not on how right she felt in his arms they'd both get through this.

He wished more than anything he could think of something that would make all the pain she was feeling disappear. He wanted to see that spitfire spark return to her eyes, that expression—so uniquely hers—that brought her face to life.

She nuzzled closer and he could feel her warm breath on his neck. The sensation sent waves of fire coursing through him. Then she looked up at him, her eyes impossibly green and her lips too full to resist. And for a fleeting moment he wanted nothing more than to taste her lips, but he caught himself.

If she hadn't been so fragile, he just might've given into that urge for just one taste of those lips. But he pulled back, putting some distance between them.

Early the next morning, before the rest of the house stirred, Sophie worked at her potting bench in the mudroom.

The cozy area was one of the reasons she'd rented the house after the divorce.

She'd envisioned a morning like this when snow frosted the windowpanes and it was too cold to go outside and putter in the yard. Here, she could ground herself by putting her hands in the earth, but be inside where the ground wasn't frozen and the windchill factor didn't threaten hypothermia.

The only thing was, her initial vision hadn't included the sickening feeling induced by the recent trio of disasters: catching Savannah in a compromising position with that boy, the revelation of the great family secret and losing Laura.

Her heart ached as she steeped a cup of Earl Grey and lit a fire in the fireplace. The dazed aftershock of the three blows tangled and sat heavy in the pit of her stomach.

How would anything ever be the same?

Her mind skittered back to how being in Luc's arms yesterday felt like a safe haven. But that wasn't real. Death was real; the possibility of Savannah ruining her life was real; the visit from King Bertrand was real.

Luc was just doing his job, and she shouldn't read anything more into it. She set down her tea and prepared to get her hands dirty.

As she coaxed a philodendron out of its terra-cotta pot onto her workbench's newspaper-covered surface, she tried to sort out her jumbled emotions, gently tending to the plant that was dangerously close to dying from its root-bound condition.

Hmm, maybe she was suffering from the same problem as the plant. She'd inextricably rooted herself to this life in Trevard that seemed to keep going from bad to worse.

Laura's sad face, the way she'd looked as she disappeared out the door on Friday flashed in her mind.

Sophie squeezed her eyes shut, trying to block out the image, but all she managed to do was remind herself how tired she was. The kind of tired that weighed you down but wouldn't let you sleep.

She'd tossed and turned again last night, awaking intermittently wondering if she'd only done things differently, if she'd seen to Laura rather than sending her away maybe the woman would still be alive.

But she hadn't, and there was no going back to correct this mistake. Tears burned her eyes, but her hands were covered.

As she thought about Laura, the problems with Savannah and St. Michel loomed in the back of her mind, like ghosts whispering a foreboding warning not to put off dealing with the problems or, as with Laura, they would come to a bad end.

Do something.

Act.

Make things right. Now.

She had two choices: sending Luc away and going back to work tomorrow, back to Mary's berating and a dead-end job. Savannah would go back to school, back to Tick and plenty of unsupervised time for God knew what; or she could take a leave of absence (if Mary would grant her one) and she could go to St. Michel for a *visit*.

Nothing said she and Savannah had to stay.

"Good morning."

Luc stood in the doorway, holding a foam cup, and looking so delicious it set off a strange tingling in the pit of her stomach.

She inhaled sharply against the sensation.

"Good morning." She focused on her hands and brushed the dirt off, a little embarrassed that the potting soil was caked under her nails. She curled her fingers inward to hide the mess. "You didn't have to buy coffee out. We have plenty here."

He took a sip and shrugged. "It was early and I didn't want to make noise in the kitchen. Are you feeling better this morning?"

She could feel his gaze on her, and she didn't even have to look up to know that he was looking at her in that way that made her think of things she hadn't contemplated in a very long time. If she let her thoughts run away with her, she imagined he was thinking the very same things.

She turned back to her potting bench and chose a bigger pot for the philodendron.

"Somewhat."

Or maybe it was the grief and exhaustion making her delirious? Making her imagine one minute that a maddeningly handsome and sophisticated European dignitary who worked for her grandfather was on a mission to seduce her.

Was she nuts?

Of course he'd do anything—including using the power of seduction—to convince her that returning to St. Michel was the right thing to do.

She shouldn't take it personally, especially not in the personal direction her newly awakened libido was leading her. Thank goodness her better judgment had been intact last night when, at the last minute, she'd pulled out of his arms and excused herself. She'd actually thought for a delusional moment that he might kiss her.

She glanced at his lips and was suddenly warm again. Given the way everything had been crashing and burning around her, she knew better than to go…there.

"I had a thought," he said. "What if you set up a trust fund for Laura's children?"

She poured potting soil into the terra-cotta pot.

"It's a nice thought," she said. "I could spare a little each month, but I can barely make ends meet as it is. It certainly wouldn't be anything grand enough to call a trust fund, but it really is a good idea."

He smiled, and her stomach dipped. She didn't want to like him. Not like *that*. She was fine when he kept his distance and didn't hold her when she was upset or try to do nice things, but darn it, she was struggling here. She had enough to worry about without his making her want something else she couldn't have. In her life, she'd built too many castles on shifting sand.

She dug a little hole in the soil, put the plant in it and covered the roots with the dirt.

"I have my resources," he said. "As the future queen of St. Michel, so will you. You could make sure those boys were well cared for, if you so chose."

"Is this a bribe? So you can get your way and get me to agree to come back to St. Michel? If so, you're not playing fair."

He pursed his lips and shrugged in that way of his that made her feel so unsophisticated, as if he were humoring her and at any moment would burst out laughing at her lack of social grace. Then again, if he did that, he wouldn't exactly be exhibiting social grace, either.

Why did she let him make her so nervous?

To get back on solid footing, she thought of Laura's four little boys. They were so young to be without a mother, relying on the charity of relatives who may not be any better off than Laura was.

She narrowed her eyes and studied Luc's expression to see if he was joking. But why would he joke about something like that?

Here she was in a real position to help. How could she just turn her back on them?

"I think it would be wonderful if we could do that," she said.

He nodded.

"How soon can we do it?" she asked.

"How soon can you be ready to leave?"

"Don't answer my question with a question."

"Well, that's part of it," he said.

"So you are trying to blackmail me."

"It would be a despicable thing to do."

"Yes, it would."

"Would it be any better for you to turn your back on a nation?"

"That's not fair. It's hardly the same thing. St. Michel will not cease to exist if I refuse to become the heir to the throne. No one there will go hungry or be homeless or mistreated without me. In fact, seeing that I know nothing about running a country, the nation might be better off without me."

"How much did you want to put in the trust?"

"What?" The non sequitur threw her.

"For the boys—how much?"

She decided to call his bluff. "I want those little guys to be well taken care of for the rest of their lives."

"Done."

She blinked. "Excuse me?"

"I'll need contact information and the name of a bank in which to set up the trust."

"Are you—are you joking?"

His face was serious now. "Absolutely not. I want you to see the great things you are capable of doing as the future queen of St. Michel. As for the nation being better off without you, I don't think so. You will have time to work with your grandfather, to learn his ways and means. It's in your blood, Sophie Baldwin. After yesterday, I just hope that you recognize that life is too short to waste, especially once your destiny comes calling."

He smiled at her and his gaze lingered in an intense way that made her knees weaken and her belly flutter.

Then he turned and walked away, leaving her speechless. Literally. Standing there with dirty hands and her mouth agape.

A trust fund for Laura's boys. Done. With a virtual wave of her hand. Well, that certainly put a new spin on everything.

Her knees were a little weak and her head was spinning, not in a way that made her feel as if she might pass out, but with possibilities.

Maybe she could make a difference.

A real difference.

She steadied herself with a deep breath. High on possibility, she made her way to the kitchen to wash her hands.

Rose was in there making a pot of coffee and taking things out of the refrigerator for breakfast. She set a carton of eggs on the table and looked at Sophie with a sorrowful expression that seemed to add years to the woman's already advanced age.

Sophie didn't say anything as she washed the grime from her hands. She only thought about this woman who had raised her so well, with so much love that Sophie never had an inkling she was adopted.

Life was short.

Luc's parting words echoed in her heart.

Yes, life *was* short.

She dried her hands and went over to Rose and put her arms around the woman.

"I'm sorry for getting so angry."

The woman gasped, a gentle intake of air that spoke more of relief than surprise, and clung tight to Sophie. "I'm so sorry," she said, hanging on to her daughter for dear life. "I'm so very sorry."

"*Shh,* you're not to blame. No one is to blame."

Her parents might have kept the truth from her, but that didn't take away from the good life they'd given her. They would *always* be her parents—her family—no matter the circumstances. She shouldn't be angry with her parents for their loyalty to the king.

They'd always showered her with unconditional love and they deserved her unconditional love in return.

As she held her mother, it all snapped into focus….

King Bertrand's talking about a dynasty coming to an end when he died; Sophie hanging on to a job where even taking the smallest steps felt like an uphill climb…

Life was short.

The move would be hard on Savannah, but it was the best chance she had of giving her daughter a good life.

Chapter Five

The fire felt nice. It warmed the living room, making it a sanctuary against the bitter cold.

Luc handed Sophie a mug of coffee and settled into a chair next to the hearth, warming his hands on his cup.

She'd asked him in here so they could talk privately, away from Rose and John, who, he was sure, would still find a way to listen.

He was certain Sophie wanted to discuss establishing the trust for the Hastings boys, but she suddenly had a different air about her. She'd washed away the potting soil grime and donned a smart pair of wool trousers and a pink cashmere sweater that brought out the pretty blush in her cheeks. She seemed stronger, more serious and pulled together than she'd been since he arrived.

She settled on the couch across from him and lifted the mug to her full lips and blew to cool the hot liquid.

Off-limits, he reminded himself. The princess of St. Michel, his boss's granddaughter, was one hundred percent off-limits. Good thing he hadn't lost control yesterday when he was tempted to kiss her.

How in the world would he have explained himself? A moment of weakness? That inappropriate relations ran in the family?

He blinked away the thought.

"How do you tolerate such inclement weather?" he asked, searching for a lighter note. "On the coldest day in St. Michel, temperatures rarely fall below fifty degrees. When that happens, it's deep winter for us."

She arched a brow.

"This isn't typical. It gets cold, but usually not this bad. Maybe it would be a good time to get away from all this snow and ice and see if winters in St. Michel really are as nice as you claim."

He studied her for a moment, trying to determine what she meant. If, in fact, this conversation was leading where he hoped.

"Are you considering a visit?" he kept his voice even, not allowing emotion to color his words.

She smiled. "How soon can we leave?"

"Tomorrow if you wish. I'll make arrangements."

"I hope you're happy," Savannah wailed. "My life is ruined. This is my last year of middle school and you're taking away everything I've worked for these seven years."

"We're just going for a visit," Sophie offered.

The girl scowled.

"Can I stay with Dad while you go, so I won't miss school?" she added, an obvious afterthought.

"Your dad is in California. What would be the difference of your going there or to St. Michel? You'd still miss school."

"In Cali, at least they'd speak the same language I do. Dad will come here. Watch, I'll call him."

It was against her better judgment to let Savannah make the call. There was no way Frank would drop everything to come back to Trevard. But the girl was already dialing.

"Savannah, please, you can't tell him about King Bertrand's visit. We're not ready for anyone to know about what's happened—about my real business in St. Michel. I may not even stay and if that's the case *no one* can ever find out that we're related to the royal family. It would just be chaos. Just tell Dad that Grandma and Grandpa are taking me there to reconnect with relatives."

She wasn't sure her daughter was listening. "Savannah, did you hear me?"

The girl turned her back on Sophie. "Daddy? Hi! It's me, Savannah."

Sophie held her breath, resisting the urge to yank the phone out of her daughter's hand until she promised to keep the secret—or at least acknowledged that Sophie had spoken to her.

"I'm fine! How are you? Oh my God, I miss you so much!" The smile in the girl's voice brought Sophie's anger down a peg. But still, this was important—

She walked around so that she and Savannah faced each other. Tried to look at her eye to eye, but she couldn't connect with her daughter's gaze. "Savannah," she stage-whispered. "Please. You don't understand how important it is that you not tell your father why we're going. I'm not asking you to lie to him, just—"

Savannah waved her mother away and stuck her finger in her ear.

Arrrrrrrrggh! Sophie wanted to scream—

"Well, the reason I'm calling is because Grandma and Grandpa want to take Mom on this really boring vacation to St. Michel." She rolled her eyes. "You know, that little place where they're from. There's like relatives there or something. Well, it sounds so-o totally boring. I was wondering if you'd come and stay with me here in Trevard while she's gone so that I don't have to go and, you know, miss all that school. You and I could like hang out. 'Cause I really miss you—"

Sophie blew out the breath she'd been holding as she realized Savannah had heard her and was doing exactly as she'd asked. Since the divorce decree stated neither she nor Frank could take their daughter out of the country without permission from the other, the call had to be made before they left. Better now than later, in case Frank caused a stink—despite how he most likely wouldn't come to stay with Savannah.

Still, Sophie was torn between hugging the girl and sitting her down to talk about respect. A simple "Okay, Mom. I'll do as you asked" would've gone a long way toward fostering mother-daughter relations. At least they were getting the call to Frank over with.

"She'll be gone three months," Savannah said into the phone. "Daddy, I really, really miss you and it'll be just like old times with your staying here. Of course Mom will be gone, but—oh. Yeah. Okay, she's right here."

Looking hopeful, Savannah held out the phone to Sophie. "Dad wants to talk to you."

As Sophie took the handset, a sense of foreboding swooped down on her.

"Hello, Frank," she said, doing her best to keep her voice neutral.

"Sophie, what the hell is going on?" She could envision Frank gritting his teeth. "You know I can't pick up and leave for three months to come babysit while you go gallivanting in Europe. Why'd you even let the kid call and get her hopes up?"

Sophie glanced at Savannah who watched her with wide, eager eyes. She hightailed it into her bedroom and shut the door to spare her daughter from what was sure to come.

"Hello? Sophie, are you there?" Frank asked, sounding even more annoyed.

"Yes, Frank, I'm here. For your information, I didn't put Savannah up to calling you. Because I knew you'd find some way to break her heart."

"Oh, give me a break. You can't expect me to come all the way across the country—"

"No, Frank, I don't expect anything out of you. But since you won't come and stay, then that means I'll have to take her with me."

She cringed at the way the words sounded. But she knew that if she asked his permission—rather than pretending that taking their daughter with her was a hardship—he'd put up a stink about Savannah going to St. Michel. If she made him think it inconvenienced her, he'd fall right into step with her plan. What an idiot.

"I don't give a damn what you do, Sophie. Just leave me out of it. I can't believe you put her up to calling me to ask if you could pawn her off while you do your *thing*."

Oh! How was it that he could make everything sound so dirty? She'd said she was going to St. Michel with her parents. Yet he'd managed to imply—with one sentence—that she was going off on some tryst. "That's not why we called. Your daughter just wanted to know if for once you were willing to step up to the plate and be a man or at least be a father to her."

"I don't have to listen to this crap. It's five o'clock in the damn morning here and you wake me up to insult me. That's low, Soph, really classless."

Yeah, this from the mouth of Mr. Manners himself, but Sophie knew arguing with him would only leave her beating her head against the wall.

"Look, just tell her you can't do it and we don't even have to talk to each other. Unless you'd care to discuss child support."

The other end of the line went dead.

He'd hung up on her. The no-good, lousy son of a—

The bedroom door opened and Savannah stood there looking pale and deflated.

"I heard," she murmured.

"Oh, baby, I'm sorry."

Once again she was left holding the bag. She could either clean up Frank's mess and make excuses or devastate her daughter by telling her the truth. She just hoped Savannah hadn't heard the part where she tried to make Frank think it was a burden to take her. Because it wasn't.

"We're going to have so much fun in St. Michel. We'll get to stay in a real castle. Haven't you always wanted to stay in a *real* castle?"

Savannah looked at Sophie as if she was spouting nonsense.

"Not since I was like five years old, Mom. Look, I'm going over to Jess's house."

Sophie wanted to tell her she couldn't go. "But what about Flea? Isn't Jess mad at you for stealing her boyfriend?"

There was that look again.

"God, Mom! His name is Tick. Why can't you remember that?"

Flea? Tick? What's the difference? Weren't both blood-sucking parasites?

"She's over him," Savannah said as if Sophie should've known. "God, did you think I'd actually try to steal my best friend's boyfriend? What kind of person do you think I am?"

I don't know anymore. That's the problem. Sophie had the sensation of swimming upstream desperately trying to keep ahold of Savannah's hand, but little by little she kept slipping....

At least one of the security agents would go with her. That wouldn't even be something she could fight with Sophie about.

"Well, don't stay long. We're leaving tomorrow. I'll have to talk to Luc to find the exact itinerary. But you need to pack. Three months is a long time to be gone."

"Exactly. That's why I want to say goodbye to my friends."

Ten minutes later, the front door slammed.

"Savannah?" Sophie called from her bedroom where she'd been putting away the clean laundry Rose had folded.

The girl appeared in her room, looking flushed and breathing hard.

"What's wrong?" Sophie asked.

Savannah folded her arms and paced the length of the room before turning to Sophie and sputtering, "Jess and Tick. That's what's wrong. I showed up at Jess's and guess who was there? Tick, that's who. They're back together. Can you believe that? I can't believe I ever liked that loser or thought Jess was my friend."

Sophie tried to think of some words to comfort her.

"How soon can we leave on this trip?"

Chapter Six

The plane landed in St. Michel at nine-thirty Tuesday evening. The second Sophie set foot on land, she noticed two things: the temperature, which the pilot had informed them, was a balmy sixty-seven degrees even though it was November; and the island smelled like paradise.

Luc gestured at a black stretch limousine on the airfield. Sophie marveled as the uniformed driver bowed and opened the car door. Savannah—who was punching the buttons on her cell phone—and Sophie's parents piled in. They took the seat that faced backward.

"After you," Luc cupped her elbow to steady her as she climbed in the car. In somewhat of a daze, Sophie found herself in the seat facing her parents. Luc slid into the vacant space next to her, popped the cork on a bottle of Krug Clos du Mesnil champagne and poured some sparkling cider for Savannah.

When everyone had a glass, Luc raised his for a toast.

"Welcome, Sophie and Savannah. Welcome back, John and Rose."

It had been more than thirty-three years since Rose and John had set foot on the island, and Sophie was torn between watching them toast each other and savoring her first glimpse of this place she might very well rule one day.

The enormity of the thought made her shudder.

Thank goodness Luc began pointing out sights of interest and spouting off facts such as "St. Michel covers an area of 197 hectares."

Hectares?

"Which would be approximately 487 acres."

Oh.

And "The *Palais de St. Michel* was built in the thirteenth century. The exterior of the castle still resembles the original thirteenth-century fortress, but the inside has been renovated and updated with the most modern of security and conveniences," he said. "It has ninety-five offices, seventy-five bathrooms and two hundred and ten bedrooms. And employs four hundred and fifty people.

"The state rooms are open for public viewing during the summer, and since 1920, the palace courtyard has been the setting for concerts given by the St. Michel National Orchestra."

"A lot of people must visit each year," Sophie said.

"True. However the *Palais de St. Michel* isn't simply a tourist attraction and museum. It is a fully working palace and our governmental headquarters. The king is involved with the day-to-day running of St. Michel and treats the nation as a business as well as a country."

Sophie's head spun.

"Will there be a pop quiz tomorrow?" she asked, only half joking.

Luc smiled, which made his eyes crinkle at the corners in a way that caused Sophie's gaze to linger and her belly to flutter.

"Look out there." He touched her arm and his shoulder pressed into her as he leaned forward and gestured toward a harbor brimming with yachts. "That's the famous St. Michel Marina. And that large boat right there—you see? That's the *Poseidon V,* which once belonged to Stavros Andros, the Greek shipping magnate. You have heard of him?"

Sophie nodded.

"Andros was a frequent visitor to our little country. The boat was sold after his death and is currently chartered by Yves De Vaugirard, the son of Pascal De Vaugirard, St. Michel's minister of finance."

"That's a big boat," Sophie said, completely and utterly aware of the heat of Luc's arm, which, even though he'd settled back into his seat, still touched hers.

"When Andros owned the *Poseidon,* he used to display Van Goghs, Renoirs and a treasure of other Impressionist paintings on board. The boat was a virtual museum afloat on the Côte d'Azur."

"Nice."

It must have been a European trait, that tendency Luc had of invading her personal space.

The car turned right and Sophie, lost in the masculine feel of his hard muscles, didn't fight the gravity that made her body lean into him a little bit more.

When the car straightened, neither of them reclaimed

their personal space. And for just a moment she wondered what the rest of his body would feel like pressed against hers—flesh to flesh…

"Are there any specific places you would like to visit?" he asked.

Oh, you have no idea.

She nodded, but she couldn't look at him because her cheeks were flaming. "The beach and the National Gallery."

"We'll come back so you can become intimately acquainted with each of them."

Intimately acquainted…that's the best idea I've heard since—

"My phone doesn't work here." Savannah's grousing pulled Sophie back, out of the world of van Goghs, Renoirs and world-class yachts, reminding her of the whirlwind it had been getting to St. Michel."

"I'm sorry there wasn't time to switch the service before we left," Sophie said, suddenly wondering what else she'd left undone.

"I'll have that taken care of in short order." Luc's words were for Sophie. "I'm at your service."

He seemed at home here. The master of this very expensive universe. As if he'd be able to make just about anything possible. And he probably could. Whereas Sophie didn't even know the location of the closest bathroom or where to buy a toothbrush if she'd forgotten to pack hers.

She racked her brain to remember if she had.

Leaving early Tuesday morning hadn't left time to take care of much but the essentials before they departed. Sunday was a blur of packing and battening down the house for three months of what was proving to be a harsh winter.

Monday at work, Sophie had to explain to Mary that she needed a leave of absence without telling her the *real* reason. All she could say was, "It's a family emergency."

And it was.

She certainly couldn't confide that the balance of the House of Founteneau rested on her shoulders. Even if she had, knowing Mary, that probably wouldn't have been reason enough to justify a leave of absence.

When they talked, Sophie's justification for the leave sounded hedgy even to her own ears. Mary asked if a family member was sick or dying and Sophie said no because she didn't want to lie.

In the end, of course, Mary, irritated and harried, turned down her request and leveled an ultimatum; "Be in the office tomorrow at eight o'clock sharp or you're fired."

Fired?

She'd never been fired from anything. Unless you counted her marriage…

Mary left Sophie no option but to spend the rest of Monday composing her letter of resignation (which Mary accepted with near glee that she didn't even try to disguise) and contacting her clients to say goodbye, assuring them they'd be in good hands.

Dear God, she hoped they'd be well taken care of, that whoever Mary hired would look out for their best interests rather than the bottom line.

Better than Sophie had done with Laura in the end.

Laura's family wasn't having a memorial service for her in Trevard. They were having her cremated and flown to California where they'd "take care of things," as Mary had so bluntly put it.

It was over.

Finished.

Not our problem anymore, Mary had said so matter-of-factly.

Exhaustion seemed to seep into her bones, and Sophie leaned against the limo window—away from Luc and his hard body, and all that talk of shipping magnates and floating museums and getting intimately acquainted—and watched the city whiz by in a blur of golden and white lights set against the indigo sky.

St. Michel looked like an exquisite Fabergé egg.

Oh, she was so out of her league.

When they reached the back security gates of the *Palais de St. Michel,* the sentries waved them through. It wasn't the first glimpse of the castle that Luc wished for Sophie. In fact, they were inside the understated back entrance and secured in the bowels of the castle so fast, she probably didn't get a proper look.

The amber half light cast shadows on her face, accentuating her cheekbones and full lips. How beautiful, he thought. Classic, unadulterated beauty.

She was just what St. Michel needed.

He wasted no time ushering Sophie and his other three charges out of the limo and unceremoniously into an elevator, which carried them directly to the living quarters—a wing of the house never open to the public.

The staff had been told only that four important guests would arrive but were given no details of who they were or their business at the castle.

He turned to Sophie to tell her as much and saw the utter exhaustion on her face and decided to spare her further briefing—at least for tonight.

Soothing classical music filtered into the lift, filling the silence as the car carried them up to the third floor. Even after the long flight, she still looked beautiful, he thought.

When the elevator doors opened, two women in gray maid's uniforms stood at the ready. "Monsieur, Madame, this is your floor," Luc said to John and Rose. "Beatrice and Rochelle will show you to your room."

Rose and John exchanged good-nights with Sophie and Savannah, hugging them and promising they'd be in good hands with Luc. As the doors closed and the lift climbed one more floor to the royal family's quarters, Sophie looked vulnerable standing there, and a little taken aback when she saw the staff of twelve that lined the elevators in two rows of six, when they finally reached her floor.

As they stepped off the elevator, Sophie looked first at Luc, then at the staff, then around at the expansive hallway. Savannah hung back slightly clinging to her mother's arm.

"This is Sophie Baldwin and her daughter, Savannah," he said. "They are very special guests of King Bertrand. I trust you will make them feel at home and treat them with the same respect as any other person who has ever occupied these quarters."

Luc found Sophie's wide-eyed expression endearing. He gave the reception area a cursory glance—from the ornate crystal chandeliers that hung from the thirty-foot ceiling, down the white and gold walls, to the marble floors—trying to see it through Sophie's eyes. The statues, mirrors and gilding must have looked extraordinary.

And quite daunting to someone who wasn't used to it. It was nice to notice it again through fresh eyes.

"Thank you," he said to the staff. "For now, I shall escort Madame Baldwin and Savannah to their apartment."

He dismissed the crew with a nod.

"This way." He led Sophie and her daughter down the hall to a set of large guilded double doors. The two hung back.

"This is where you will stay," he said. "I took the liberty of putting the two of you in the same apartment. I figured you'd be more comfortable that way. But if you'd prefer, Savannah can have her own quarters."

"No!" they both said simultaneously.

"I mean, thank you," Sophie said. "But I'd prefer that Savannah stay here with me."

The girl nodded.

"Very well, the apartment contains six bedrooms, so you should have plenty of room."

"Six bedrooms?" Savannah asked. "Are you kidding me?"

"No, I'm not," Luc said. "All for your mother and you. You may choose three for you and three for your mother."

"Whoa!" With that, the girl took off down the hall, calling something about *dibs.*

Sophie laughed and crossed her arms over the front of her. "You'll have to excuse her—well, both of us actually. This is a little overwhelming for both of us. This *apartment,* as you call it, is twice the size of my house."

Her humility was touching, a breath of fresh air in this climate of women who would stop at nothing to get what they wanted.

"Only the best for the *princesses* of St. Michel."

Sophie dipped her head, but not before he noticed the color that bloomed in her cheeks.

"I know you're tired," she said, glancing up at him without raising her chin. "But will you come in? Please?"

The request seemed more of a plea than an initiation. A protective impulse unfurled inside him.

"Of course. I was hoping you'd give me the honor of giving you the grand tour. It's a special place. This is where Princess Sylvie lived."

She looked up at him with large, astonished eyes.

"The apartment has been closed off for many years, but King Bertrand decided to open it for you and Savannah—you are his family," Luc said. "I'm sure you're eager to see your mother's room."

Silently they walked side by side, through the expansive hallway, stopping at a set of double doors nearly as large as the ones in the front entryway. Luc snared Sophie's wide gaze before opening them, revealing a room that continued the gilded and white theme of the apartment, but with added touches of pink velvet and ceilings that rivaled the Sistine Chapel.

Sophie stood at the door as if she was afraid to enter. Luc cupped her elbow and led her inside.

"This was her room, and if you think you'll be comfortable here, it can be yours. Please, have a look around."

He stepped out into the hallway, leaving Sophie alone to explore. A few moments later she joined him.

"Okay, I take back what I said before. The *bathroom* in there is bigger than my house. The rest of this is just…"

She shook her head and ran a hand through her hair.

"A little overwhelming?" he asked.

She nodded.

He understood how he felt. It was overwhelming to him in a different sort of way. He'd spent much of his youth in this apartment, when Antoine and the royal family lived here. In fact, he hadn't been inside since the king had moved his family to the apartment he was in now.

"Where do you live?" she asked. "Are we neighbors? Do you have your own mansion inside this castle down the hall?"

She made a fluttering gesture with her hand and smiled. A dimple in her right cheek that he'd never noticed before winked at him. How had he missed that?

"I have a house about two kilometers from the palace. If you need me, no matter what time of day or night, I insist you call."

In a flash of irrational thought, he hoped she would somehow need him…

Savannah trotted up alongside her mother. "Oh. My. God. Mom, can you believe this place? I mean it…it's like Cinderella's castle."

Subdued by the random intimacies that kept permeating his thoughts, he knew it was time to leave.

"I'm sure you and Savannah would like to get settled in and get a good night's sleep. King Bertrand plans to present you to the Crown Council tomorrow."

Sophie's throat worked.

"Really?" she asked. "I don't know if that's such a good idea, because I'm still not sure we'll be able to stay…permanently."

She was exhausted, he thought, and that's what was contributing to her hesitancy.

"Perhaps I can convince the king to delay the meeting a day or so. To give you time to adjust."

He hoped it was exhaustion talking, because now that she was here, he couldn't imagine this place without her. Sophie Baldwin was exactly what St. Michel needed.

Chapter Seven

Miraculously Sophie slept through the night.

It wasn't exactly restful, more like a strange dream-filled sleep, of swirling images of Luc leading her through a labyrinthine castle. In the dream, she couldn't find her daughter, but the king kept insisting that she *move forward, that she keep going.*

Sophie sat up and blinked at the sunlight streaming in through the French doors on the wall and saw Savannah snuggled down under the pink satin duvet next to her in the expansive four-poster bed.

She sighed with tender relief and fell back onto the pillows.

Sometime in the middle of the night, Savannah must have crawled into bed with her. Maybe she'd had the same unsettling dreams?

Probably not. They were far away from home in this

strange old castle. That could be sort of unsettling for a girl…of any age. She reached out and smoothed a lock of dark brown hair off her daughter's forehead.

Savannah stirred but didn't awaken.

Sophie carefully removed her hand, returning it to the cool of the buttery soft, white cotton sheets.

The events of the past week seemed almost as unreal as the bizarre images she'd dreamed of last night.

But here they were. This castle, this bedroom in this sprawling apartment were as real as could be.

What was it like for Princess Sylvie to grow up in this *Palais de St. Michel?* She tried to picture her in this very room.

Had this been Sylvie's bed? She ran her hands over the sheets—obviously new or at least not thirty-three years old. The place smelled like furniture polish and old money. Sophie's gaze scanned the gilded room. On the bedside table sat a black-and-white photo of the young princess.

This was her *birth mother*…a woman she knew next to nothing about aside from the glorified wild-child legends spun by the paparazzi. It was the most incongruent feeling looking at a picture of a young woman who was familiar, yet nearly as two-dimensional and far removed as one of the goddesses painted on the ceiling above her bed.

Sophie stared at the photo and tried to imagine Sylvie as a living, breathing girl sitting at the Louis XIV dressing table getting ready for…for…a night out with Nick Morrison, the celebrated bad-boy rocker?

Nick Morrison?

Sophie let her arm fall over her eyes and tried to see Sylvie and Nick as parents. *Her* parents. But it just didn't fit.

She could almost see it, but it was absolutely, positively too much for her to wrap her head around.

Her mind kept superimposing a famous shot of Sylvie—one of her in a 1970s Paris disco, smoking a cigarette with her long, straight dark hair framing her face, her dramatic eyes done up in Cleopatra-like fashion. The shot was so overused by the media it had become the defining image of the young woman who had been just three years older than Savannah when she died.

Sophie's heart pinched at the thought.

She sat up and hugged her knees to her chest. Then as she reached out to pick up the framed photo off the nightstand, someone knocked on the door. Sophie's hand flinched away. She half expected museum security to burst in and demand she not touch the *objets d'art*.

Instead, a slight woman dressed in a gray maid's uniform hesitantly pushed open the door.

"*Excusez-moi, s'il vous plaît,* Madame Baldwin. Monsieur Lejardin is here to see you."

Sophie's heart hammered.

"Just a moment," she whispered. "Don't let him in just yet." She got out of bed carefully so as not to wake Savannah, raked her hands through her hair and swiped at the sleep in her eyes. The thought of Luc catching her drowsy and sleep-rumpled was far worse than museum security bursting in.

"He is waiting in the dining room and would very much appreciate a word with you as you enjoy your breakfast. After you make yourself ready."

"Oh. Of course."

Sophie stood awkwardly in bare feet and the borrowed silk

nightgown someone had laid out for her the night before, unsure of how to dismiss the woman.

"Hmm...*merci beaucoup.*"

The maid nodded and left.

Right. As if he'd be standing outside her bedroom. They weren't in Trevard any longer. They were in the *Palais de St. Michel.* Things were more formal here.

It was just that she'd gotten used to Luc always being there—right over her shoulder. Right next to her, as he'd been in the limo last night. Now that she had so much more...breathing room in this place, it was ludicrous to think Luc would continue to be a constant presence in her life. Because if he did, that would mean it was by his choice rather than out of duty.

She snuffed out the vague sense of disappointment at the thought of their going their separate ways and left Savannah to enjoy the sweet sleep of the innocent. As she headed toward the bathroom, she noticed someone had set her suitcase inside her room.

Hmm...she thought she and Savannah had been alone in the apartment last night. Although it was harmless, the thought of an unknown person creeping in as they slept gave her the heebie-jeebies.

Maybe they weren't alone, she thought as she turned on the faucet in the huge marble shower and peeled off her nightgown. The best staff was supposed to be all but invisible except when needed.

She covered herself and glanced around the bathroom. Okay, now she was just being ridiculous. Surely some things were sacred.

Still, there must be thousands of places to hide in this

castle. As a child, Sylvie must have played some marvelous games of hide-and-seek in this maze of a mansion.

Right about now Sophie wished she could discover some of those hiding places and render herself invisible while she decided whether she had it in her to accept full responsibility for what lay on the horizon.

Luc stood and bowed when Sophie entered the dining room. She looked gorgeous in classic gray tweed slacks and a black sweater that hugged those curves he found so enticing.

"Good morning," he said. "Happy Thanksgiving."

She stopped for a moment and blinked, as if she'd forgotten something.

"Good morning." She shook her head as if clearing a haze. "In all this excitement, I didn't realize today was Turkey Day. I guess I'm still messed up on time."

The room seemed to light up in her presence, he thought as he pulled out a chair for her at the dining table. As she sat, he caught a whiff of her freshly washed hair and resisted the urge to lean in closer.

Unfortunately that smile in her eyes was certain to vanish when he delivered the news that the meeting with the Crown Council was firmly set for noon.

As Luc took a seat to Sophie's right, he strengthened his resolve to lead with his head rather than falling prey to the intoxicating scent of black sweaters and shampoo.

"Did you sleep well?" he asked.

She nodded, then shrugged. "Jet lag, I guess. My inner clock's a little off. Obviously my calendar's off, too."

She laughed, a sound like fine crystal.

"I have something for you," Luc said. "Phones for you and Savannah."

He took them out of his jacket pocket and laid them on the table next to her.

She knit her brow. "There must be a mistake. These aren't our phones. We had the old Nokias—not very fashionable, I'm sure. But they do the job."

It was wonderful to be able to do this for her. Because she didn't expect it. She wasn't about flash and glamour, although her natural beauty was far more attractive than most of the women he'd met who tried so hard. Too hard.

"This a new phone that isn't even on the market yet. A friend is marketing them and he gave me a few to try. They will target iPhone customers. I figured Savannah might think it was—how do you say...cool? To be the first to own one."

Sophie looked a little taken aback. She opened her mouth to say something, stopped, then started again. "Thank you, Luc, but..." She bit her lip. "*Hmm,* this is a little embarrassing, but they are expensive."

He nodded. "I'm sure they are. Isn't it ridiculous what people will pay for a telephone? But yours is gratis. Of course the *Palais de St. Michel* has its own network. So there's no cost for service."

She looked as if she'd become instantly wide-awake. He picked up the phone with the tag that read *Sophie* and handed it to her. She slanted him a glance and hesitantly accepted it.

"I had our technology director transfer the numbers stored in your former phone. I took the liberty of having him program my number into speed dial. Please, never hesitate to call me. I am at your service."

As she bit her bottom lip, he hoped she would call, because

outside of taking care of her phones and informing her of the Crown Council meeting—which really wasn't his job; it would be her assistant's once she was set—he shouldn't call her. Not for the reasons he wanted to.

"Thank you. Savannah will be so excited."

A server entered the room and placed two large platters on the center of the table—one heaped with breakfast meats and eggs cooked in every fashion imaginable; the other held bread and pastries. The servants filled coffee cups and crystal goblets with juice—a choice of orange, grapefruit, pomegranate and tomato.

Sophie chose the freshly squeezed orange juice, but waited until Luc said, "Please, help yourself to some breakfast," to serve herself a modest helping of scrambled eggs and bacon.

He followed suit, serving himself as he weighed the best way to break the news.

"I met with King Bertrand early this morning," Luc said. "He's very glad you're here."

Sophie swallowed a bite of egg and smiled.

"This morning you've already gotten us new phones *and* had a meeting. Before breakfast. Do you ever sleep?"

That was the beauty of being organized and unencumbered. The reason he needed to focus on work and not on the scent of the *princesse's* shampoo. That's how he got things done.

"Sleep is highly overrated."

"When will I have the pleasure of seeing my dear grandfather?"

"How about today for lunch, in honor of your Thanksgiving holiday? We don't celebrate it here in St. Michel, but he thought it might be a nice way to welcome you."

"He's in luck. I just happened to have an opening in my schedule."

Her eyes twinkled and he hated to say anything that would change that, but it wouldn't be fair for her to expect an intimate lunch with her grandfather and walk into a council luncheon meeting. "Great. How about if the Crown Council and I join you?"

She frowned and set down her fork with a loud clank.

"Well, in that case, I'm busy. I mean, you're welcome to join us, but I'm not ready to meet the Crown Council."

"The king thinks it best that you're introduced today. The longer we delay, the greater the chance of word leaking. If anyone learns of this before the council has been informed, we will have a mutiny on our hands. Of course, the king is right."

And even if he wasn't, this wasn't a battle Luc wanted to fight. The meeting was inevitable. Better sooner than later.

She glared at him.

"And what if I don't come?"

"That wouldn't be a good idea."

She stared at her hands for a moment.

"Sounds like you're not giving me a choice, doesn't it?"

"We certainly won't force you to do anything against your will. However, the king is concerned that—"

He paused and glanced at the footman who stood innocuously against the wall.

"We require privacy, *s'il vous plaît*. Please leave us and close off the dining room."

The servant nodded and indicated the bell affixed to the underside of the table. "Monsieur, madame, please ring if we may serve you."

With that he disappeared.

Luc waited for him to close the doors before continuing to speak. The walls had ears, especially in a case like this, where the royal apartment had been opened and readied for *guests* for the first time since 1983 when the king had vacated the place after the loss of his wife and second daughter.

The queen had suffered a stroke and never recovered. Then just four months later, Princess Celine had died in an automobile accident. It was almost too much for the king to bear. Thus he moved himself and Prince Thibault and Prince Antoine to smaller quarters in the east wing of the palace.

Was it any wonder that opening the apartment after all these years to two Americans had caused speculation amongst the staff to run rampant?

All the more reason to introduce Sophie to the council. All the more reason to speak cautiously, even though they were supposedly alone.

He scooted his chair closer to Sophie and leaned in.

"Pardonnez-moi," he whispered, fully aware that his proximity was making her uncomfortable. She tried to scoot back, but he took her arm and refused to let her reclaim her space. "I know this is not comfortable, but this is the perfect example as to why we must not waste any time informing the Crown Council. The servants have eyes and ears. They listen and see. Even overhearing a simple conversation such as this could spell disaster if someone were to leak matters to the press before we inform the council."

She jerked her head away and he noticed her cheeks were flushed. "Yes, but—"

Luc pressed a finger to her lips. She glared up at him with a look that registered somewhere between anger and defiance.

A vaguely sensuous current passed between them. She was so close and again he was tempted to lean in and kiss those enticing lips. The tips of his fingers brushed her jawline as he removed his finger. An action that could've been interpreted as unintentional…or not.

"Meeting the council doesn't mean you must stay, although I truly hope you will."

She blinked as if surprised to hear him utter that confession. Perhaps he'd surprised himself, but this was no time to backpedal, not when he needed her to cooperate.

It was his job to ensure she cooperated, he reminded himself, determined to ignore the vibrant chord those green eyes plucked deep down in his solar plexus.

"Oh. My. God. I can't believe the new phone Luc gave me. It makes an iPhone seem like a dinosaur." Savannah flopped down next to Sophie on the brocade couch in the living room of their apartment. "I didn't know they gave presents on Thanksgiving here in St. Michel. But it's pretty cool that they do! Look, Mom, it gets Internet and television. It's got all kinds of movies and songs already loaded—oh my God! It has the new Panic at the Disco CD. It hasn't even been released."

The girl squealed, shoved an earbud in her right ear and handed Sophie the other one. Obligingly, Sophie listened to a few strains of the loud music, feeling both grateful to Luc for giving them the phones and resentful at his pushing her to meet the council before she was ready. And more than a little confused by the undeniable attraction that zinged through her every time she looked at him.

"Savannah, turn it down a little, sweetie. You're going to

ruin your hearing. Please don't turn up the volume past the halfway mark."

Much to Sophie's amazement, the girl minded her without so much as an eye roll. Maybe this getaway would do them both some good. If Sophie could just make it past the Crown Council...and the magnetic pull of Luc Lejardin.

After breakfast she'd halfheartedly agreed to attend the luncheon on the stipulation that Savannah didn't have to go.

Not yet.

Luc reluctantly agreed, asserting, however, that they'd want to meet the girl sooner or later, and it might as well be sooner.

The Crown Council just sounded so...formal and *unfriendly.* There was no reason to subject Savannah to that. What was the point of subjecting a fourteen-year-old girl to the board if they ended up going back to Trevard?

Which might happen.

She'd come to St. Michel on a fact-finding mission...for a look-see to determine if it was the right move. But this quick meeting was starting to feel like a bait and switch: *Now that we have you captive—sit here, wear this.... Ooooh, doesn't she look perfect on the throne with the crown on her head?*

"Look, Mom, I can even take pictures and record things on it. Here—" she held out the phone. "Say something."

Sophie touched her daughter's hand.

"I'm glad you're happy. Don't forget to say thank-you to Luc. He'll be here any minute."

"You bet I'll say thanks," Savannah said. "I want to hug him."

Yeah, so do I, sweetie.

* * *

Since that wasn't possible, Sophie vaguely wished for something just as exciting to look forward to—something to distract her from the ominous meeting.

What were they looking for in her?

Shouldn't experience outtrump bloodlines in the qualifications for running a country?

Right. Just as her decision to pack up and move to the other side of the Atlantic should be based on wanting to do the job, not because every time Luc's gaze met hers her heart turned over.

She'd learned her lesson the hard way with Frank, and she wouldn't make the same mistake again. Although Luc, with his Armani suits and sexy smile, was worlds different from Frank.

"Oh my God, I have voice mails—look!"

With a pale pink painted thumbnail, the girl held down the key that retrieved messages.

"One from Jess and one from…Tick? *Ugh.* Can you believe Tick had the nerve to call me after he hooked up with her again? He's an idiot if he thinks we're getting back together. I'm going to my room to call Jess. She's going to die when she hears I have the new Panic CD." Savannah stood as she dialed her phone. "Let me know when Luc gets here. Oh—Hey, Jess…It's me, Savannah. Oh. My. God. You'll never believe what's going on…."

Her voice trailed off as she walked down the hall and was finally muted by the closed bedroom door.

Sophie sat alone in the living room listening to the ticking of the antique grandfather clock, relieved that there was an ocean between her daughter and Emo Jess…and Tick. Yes, especially Tick.

When Sophie was a teenager, she and her friends had a "sisters before misters" pact, meaning they'd never date each other's exes and they'd never let a guy come between their friendship. When they left Trevard, she'd thought that Jess and Savannah's Tick tug-of-war had been such a breach of this principle that the dubious friendship was over. Then again, maybe that's where the "sisters before misters" rule applied. Tick was out. Their friendship was in.

Hmm…perhaps that was one point in favor of staying in St. Michel. Although keeping her daughter locked away in a castle, like Rapunzel, certainly wasn't the solution, either.

"Who is Savannah talking to?" Sophie started at the sound of Rose's voice.

"Hi, Mom. I didn't realize you were here."

"I just arrived." Rose sat on the wingback chair across from Sophie and crossed her ankles. "Claude let me in."

Claude? Oh, the butler, or whatever the French called a man who slipped around like a ghost—not really there, yet always there.

Sophie thought about what Luc had said at breakfast about the walls having ears and it gave her the creeps. Could she ever get used to never being alone again?

"Happy Thanksgiving, *ma chérie*." Rose kissed Sophie on the cheek.

"Happy Thanksgiving, Mom."

"Where's my granddaughter this fine morning?"

"Luc activated her phone, and she's returning calls."

Rose glanced at her watch. "She does realize there's a

seven-hour time difference between St. Michel and home, doesn't she?"

Sophie shrugged.

"It's not that early at home—well, six o'clock. If she wakes someone up, I'm sure that'll make her more conscious of the time change than anything I could say."

Rose nodded and fidgeted. She uncrossed her ankles, then recrossed them the other direction, smoothed her skirt and seemed generally restless.

"You look awfully nice," she said. "That's a beautiful outfit. What are your plans this afternoon? I was hoping you and Savannah would want a traditional Thanksgiving dinner tonight."

Sophie glanced down at the conservative navy-blue Chanel suit her maid, Adèle, had laid out for her to wear to the luncheon. Surprisingly, it fit as if it had been custom-made for her. Amazing, seeing how she'd never had a fitting. Her mother's handy work or another page from the open book of details about her life?

"What, Luc hasn't given you my itinerary? In fact, I'm surprised he didn't send you here to make sure I hadn't defected."

Actually, now that she'd voiced the thought, it held more truth than she'd initially intended.

"Did he?" Sophie asked.

"Ma chérie." Rose laid her hands in her lap, ladylike, one over the other. "I wish you would trust us."

Sophie had to bite the inside of her cheeks to keep from reminding Rose that she had trusted her. All her life. And given the circumstances she thought she was doing pretty well to have come this far.

Rose cleared her throat. "I know what you're thinking,

Sophie. I can only pray that you'll find it in your heart to truly forgive me for keeping the truth from you all these years. Please, you must know that I couldn't love you more if I had given birth to you. You are my daughter."

Sophie felt the dam start to weaken as tears threatened. After Laura's accident, she'd decided to forgive, but she and Rose hadn't had time to sit down and discuss it. "Mom, I know that and I love you, too. It's just…It's just so much, so fast. But I wonder about…"

She couldn't bring herself to say the words…to wonder aloud about Sylvie, her birth mother. It was crazy. If anyone would know, it would be Rose.

"About Sylvie?" she asked, as if reading her mind. "It's perfectly natural for you to be curious about her."

Sophie nodded and a rush of relief flooded over her.

"She was such a young, beautiful girl," Rose said. "A handful, yes, but a good girl at heart. You favor her. Have you noticed from the pictures?"

Sophie nodded and the grandfather clock struck twelve-forty-five.

"Are you ready?" Luc's voice sounded from behind her, jolting her with awareness before she even had a chance to turn around.

Rose smiled. "We will talk more later, my love. We'll have a fabulous feast tonight. Luc, you will join us, *non?*"

Sophie felt strangely shy and rooted to the sofa, but then Luc appeared at her side. He was getting awfully good at being there—in the right place. At just the right time. Just when she needed him.

"Are you ready?" He smiled and offered his hand. There was something reassuring in his steadfast strength.

She put her hand in his and stood, savoring the delicious rush.

For the first time since she'd arrived in St. Michel, Sophie felt as if she might be okay.

Because everything would be okay. She had to believe that.

Really, feeling like this, what was the worst that could happen?

Chapter Eight

She looked like a painter's study of light and shadow, Luc thought, as he led Sophie down a series of corridors toward King Bertrand's chambers.

Neither of them spoke, and it gave his mind plenty of opportunity to ponder the contrast of dark hair against creamy skin and startlingly green eyes.

She was reminiscent of a Renoir come to life.

Beautiful.

Simply stunning.

He wrenched his mind from the landscape of her beauty, opened the door to the anteroom and waited for her to enter. As she did, he noticed her earlier confidence seemed to have melted into guarded apprehension.

The door closed behind him and they were alone in the

room. He touched her shoulder. Perhaps not a professional gesture, but he wanted to reassure her.

It was his job to reassure her, to make sure she was of the state of mind to put her best foot forward to the council, but this felt more personal.

He wanted her to succeed. His hand slid down to her arm and the firm, feminine feel of her sent a jolt right down to his toes, especially when she turned toward him and they stood face-to-face.

"Everything will be fine," he reassured, taking her hands in his. "Simply be yourself."

She lowered her gaze, holding on to his hands. He was suddenly overcome with the urge to lift her hands to his lips. But when she looked back up at him, ready to say something, she gazed past him, pulling her hands from his.

"*Bonjour,* Monsieur Lejardin," said a voice from behind them—Marci, a petite brunette who served as assistant to the king's personal secretary. "King Bertrand is expecting you."

Luc stepped back. It wasn't like him to allow himself to get caught up in the moment.

As Marci walked toward an antique writing table, her gaze swept a cool, head-to-toe assessment of Sophie.

Marci picked up the telephone. "Monsieur Lejardin is here," she said into the receiver, then showed them into the room.

"Good, you're early." King Bertrand sat behind his desk writing in a journal. "I want a word with Sophie before we head to lunch."

Sophie shot Luc a panicked glance, as if he were her lifeline. Perhaps he should've better prepared her, but given the short notice, it had seemed better to verbally brief her on the various personalities of the seven-member council rather than inundate her with policies and political leanings.

Not that she couldn't have handled it, but too much, too fast would've been counterproductive.

She'd be fine, and he'd come to her aid if she needed him.

The king stood, walked over and extended his hand.

Seeing them together, the king with his granddaughter—the first woman in ages to threaten his good sense—reminded Luc of his place: he was here to serve. He was to assist Sophie, to steer her in the direction of what was right for St. Michel.

Falling for her wasn't part of that assignment. She was of royal blood and he was what amounted to the hired help.

Emotionally, he forced himself to take a big step back, distancing himself from Sophie and doing his best to ignore the ensuing pang of regret.

The moment Sophie, the king and Luc walked into the royal dining room, which vaguely resembled a scaled-down version of *Hogwarts's* great hall, seven pairs of curious eyes sized her up, then dismissed her.

She wanted nothing more than to hide under the lavishly dressed luncheon table. If it wouldn't have been so utterly undignified, she just might have done it.

Better yet, she wanted to make a run for it—grab Savannah, leave the *Palais de St. Michel* and never return.

Except that she had no idea how to find her way back to the apartment through this maze of a monstrous place, much less how to get out of this fortress. If she tried, she'd probably end up having to call Luc to come find her.

Hmm—maybe that wasn't such a bad idea...

Alas, because Luc's hand was firmly on the small of her back propelling her forward, and her legs felt like sun-warmed chocolate, it was probably in her best interest to stay. Too bad the two of them couldn't escape back into Marci's office. The way he'd held her hands as they waited had felt nice. Perhaps she was just imagining it, but she could've sworn that a current of—something—passed between them. Maybe it was wishful thinking. Or perhaps nerves. Not to mention, she hadn't yet adjusted to the seven-hour time difference.

A server appeared with a tray of champagne flutes. The king helped himself and turned to address two men who were standing near. Luc lifted two glasses off the tray, handed one to Sophie and raised his glass to her.

"Santé!"

Whatever had or hadn't passed between them, his presence was reassuring and she focused on him rather than the fact that she was the only woman amidst this group of downright grumpy-looking old men. Well, Luc wasn't old, and really neither was the guy to the king's left, the one who looked as if he smelled something foul.

She glanced around the room taking in the aristocratic opulence—the dark polished wood, the intricate tapestries that adorned the walls, the lavishly set luncheon table. It was like something from a dream—or Hearst Castle, where you were supposed stay behind the velvet ropes.

Yet here she was on the inside; heiress to…all this?

At least Luc was close by. That made her feel better. He was proving to be the one constant in this ever-shifting sea of change.

How strange that he was part of this exclusive inner circle, yet worlds different. And it wasn't simply the age difference. The others had a completely different vibe—a stuffy self-importance that smacked of calculation and hidden agendas.

Maybe it wasn't right to peg them before she'd even been introduced, but it didn't take a genius to know that a person didn't get a seat on the Crown Council without some political clout.

"Sophie," said the king. "I would like you to meet my godson and fellow council member, Vicomte Yves De Vaugirard."

He gestured to the thin man on his left, the one who looked as if he smelled poo.

"Yves, allow me to introduce Sophie Baldwin."

Now that they'd been formally introduced, it appeared as though the stench he smelled had worsened. The *vicomte*— no less—was probably in his early- to mid-fifties, Sophie guessed, or maybe not even. Maybe it was his pinched look that aged him.

"Comte De Vaugirard, Yves's father and the senior member of the council, is over there." The king gestured with his head at a man across the room. "They are from one of St. Michel's oldest and most respected families.

"Yves, I trust you will entertain Sophie with anecdotes about our great nation," the king prompted.

"But of course. I welcome any opportunity to brag about my beloved St. Michel." After her grandfather disengaged and wandered off to join another conversation, Yves measured Sophie over the top of his champagne flute, as if weighing whether he should divulge inside information on an exclusive club in which she didn't stand a chance of joining.

Yves took a long, bored draw of his aperitif before he began. "Of course we are one of the best examples of a nation benefiting by betting on the rich rather than the poor. The proletariat make up but a minute segment of the population. Because of that, we have very little poverty—and what little we do have is so small it's hardly an issue. It has been so for centuries."

Okay. And what was she supposed to say to that?

Oh, bravo. The poor are such nuisances.

"Ah, but Yves, did you mention the high literacy rate and the emphasis on education?" Luc pressed. "That's a contributing factor to the high standard of living. You make it sound like we're an elitist society."

She loved how Luc didn't simply go along with the *vicomte's* party line. That he challenged what sounded exactly like elitist propaganda.

Yves sniffed, then turned to say something in French to the man standing next to him. Sophie might have worried that he was talking about her, but really there was no chance of that.

She wasn't even on the Vicomte De Vaugirard's radar.

Luc leaned in and whispered, "A regular humanitarian, isn't he? My brother, Henri, is the minister of art, culture and education and he takes pride in our country's high literacy rate. I like to remind the Crown Council of the good job he does every chance I get."

He winked and their gazes snared. Something about the Mr. Darcy-esque look combined with the velvet of his French accent caused the jumble of butterflies in her stomach to swoop in one big spiraling loop.

And for a moment she feared she was in trouble, but in the nick of time the king made his way to the table and everyone followed.

"Take the seat to the king's right," Luc whispered, as if

nothing had transpired between them. Maybe nothing had—not now or earlier in Marci's office. At least not on Luc's part. Maybe it was just her imagination. And if so, it was probably best left at that.

Still, she was relieved when he claimed the empty place next to her. With his prompting, she might not make a total fool of herself.

Or so she thought until a server rushed up and yanked Sophie's napkin off her plate with a flourish, and placed it in her lap. Should she have done that immediately after she sat down?

But other liveried servants gave the council members the same treatment. Sophie relaxed a little, remembering a trick she'd learned in a high school etiquette class where you put your hands in your lap and discreetly touched the thumb and forefingers to make the "okay" sign on each hand. If you looked more closely, the fingers on the left hand formed a lowercase *b,* indicating your *bread plate* was on the left; the fingers on the right hand formed a lowercase *d,* indicating your *drink* was on the right.

Okay, so it worked best at crowded round luncheon tables where the place settings tended to bump one into the next. Here—at this expansive rectangular table—each person had plenty of room. It was obvious which components of the place setting were hers.

Too bad she didn't have more Miss Manners tricks up her sleeve. She'd just have to make do with the basics, like not talking with her mouth full, which probably wouldn't be a temptation, because no one but Luc seemed the least bit interested in what she had to say.

That was fine with her.

Too bad they couldn't take the bottle of champagne and get out of here….

She stole a glance at Luc, who'd been ensnared in conversation by the man to his right.

She smiled to herself. Contemplating the places she and Luc could go was a thought that just might sustain her through what was otherwise proving to be a torturous afternoon.

*Okay…*obviously she'd had enough bubbly.

"Madame Baldwin has experience working in social services for her county in North Carolina," Luc said in an attempt to draw her into the conversation with the council member to his right—*Oh, what was his name? The introductions had been fast, the accents thick and the champagne flowing freely. Geesh, if this was a working lunch, how the heck did anyone get any work done around here?*

The councilman nodded and engaged in another conversation with the bald man across the table. Still, social services was something familiar, something she could discuss intelligently, and because Luc had mentioned it, she said, "Earlier, the *vicomte* mentioned that a small segment of the population lived in poverty? Who are these people and does the government do anything to help them?"

The bald man across the table surprised her by answering, "It's a sad fact, but most of our country's poorest are employees of the *Palais de St. Michel.* Still, I suppose that one could view it as the government helping them by giving them work, no matter how meager."

She was so startled by the quip that for a moment she was speechless. Then the king raised his glass in a toast.

"I'm very happy that we are all together today," he said. "I've called this *Thanksgiving* luncheon rather than a regular meeting in chambers because it's a very special occasion. One, in fact, that will give each of us a reason to be thankful. Before I get to that, I would like to introduce you to Madame Sophie Baldwin. As I requested in the bulletin you received, we will conduct this meeting in English for Madame Baldwin's benefit. Later, I will tell you more about her and why she's here today. But first we shall eat."

A legion of servers appeared with covered trays and did a synchronized revealing of the first course: *foie gras.*

Eat? Oh, sure.

How could she eat this lavish meal when the person serving her might be living in poverty? She felt like Marie Antoinette.

Even if Sophie had no stomach for lunch, King Bertrand ate with enough zeal for both of them, quickly polishing off his duck liver and knocking back two glasses of Beaujolais.

All around her she heard snippets of conversation: a world leader's name mentioned here, quips about foreign policy and alternative energy sources over there. She wanted to revisit the question of St. Michel's poor—did they have enough to eat? Adequate health care?

As she glanced around—at the king, who seemed lost in his own culinary nirvana, and the other men who comprised the counil—it suddenly hit her that *they* were the power behind the throne.

They weren't looking to her, as heir to the throne, to "run" the country—oh no, that was their job. They needed a figure-head. Someone to sit on the float and wave while the council steered.

Of course.

She wasn't sure if that realization made it better or worse.

Could she ever be content to sit passively, while the rich and powerful did the work and *turned a blind eye* to a small, yet *très* undesirable segment of the population whose only crime was that they were poor?

The thought weighed heavy as the entrée (read: appetizer) gave way to the *plat principal* (read: entrée) of terrine de saumon aux épinards (salmon and spinach terrine)—not exactly traditional Thanksgiving fare, but it was fine since they were having turkey and the trimmings that night. The salmon was followed by a salad, which was cleared for the cheese course and finally a delicious crème caramel and café. But for some strange reason, they didn't serve the café with the dessert; it came afterward.

"And how is it that French women don't get fat?" Sophie murmured as she sipped her coffee.

"Fat?" Luc looked confused. "You have nothing to worry about. You look fabulous."

"Thank you." She hadn't meant to say it out loud. "I wasn't fishing for a compliment. I was just referencing the book...." She was suddenly drowsy from the food and wine and weary from always trying to explain herself. If one thing had become clear today it was that Luc was on her side. And she couldn't think of anyone she'd rather have in her corner.

"You know what? Never mind. Thank you for the compliment. I'll take it."

He smiled, that sexy, lazy smile of his. "As you should."

He looked as if he wanted to say more, but King Bertrand was tapping his dessert spoon against his champagne flute, calling his council to order. In a matter of moments her secret would be revealed.

Chapter Nine

After Sophie's introduction, the Crown Council meeting disbanded abruptly. Good thing, Luc thought, because Sophie did not need to hear the inevitable fallout sung by a chorus of bruised egos.

He escorted her back to her apartment and returned to the council chambers for a meeting Pascal and Yves De Vaugirard had demanded with the king. He hadn't been invited, but because he was already deeply involved, he thought King Bertrand could use some backup. As minister of protocol, he wouldn't be entirely out of place.

When Luc walked in, Yves stopped midtirade and turned his venom on him.

"What the hell are you doing here? This is a private meeting between Crown Council members and the king. Get out."

King Bertrand slammed his fist down on the table. "Nobody gives orders in this office but me. Monsieur Lejardin will stay."

The elder De Vaugirard stiffened and the younger glared at Luc like a cobra poised to strike. Seated in the two chairs in front of the king's desk, both emanated an aura of mutinous revulsion. The only difference was that the father was better at disguising his than the son was. Nonetheless, Luc still picked up on it.

"If you think you can pull that commoner out of the woodwork and install her as heiress to the throne, you're more senile that I thought."

"Yves, that will do." Pascal didn't flinch as he reprimanded his son. "You must remember with whom you are speaking. He is the king of St. Michel and you will treat him with due respect."

Yves leaned forward and spat through gritted teeth, "I don't care if you are the king, you're in violation of the St. Michel constitution. Even *you* cannot get away with that."

A bad feeling urged Luc to slip his hand inside his jacket pocket to his holstered gun, ready to draw if need be.

King Bertrand stood, fire blazing in his dark, watery eyes. He pointed toward the door. "Get out or I'll see you impeached from the council."

Yves did not move, but Pascal was on his feet in an instant, trying to smooth the king's ruffled feathers.

"Here, here, we've behaved irrationally, Your Majesty. Please, forgive us. We're just a bit…overwhelmed by the news you've bestowed upon us today."

"Would you like me to escort Vicomte De Vaugirard to the door?" Luc offered, itching for the opportunity to throw him out on his ass.

"You lay one hand on me and I'll—"

"Yves!" Comte De Vaugirard glowered at his son, who'd redirected his venomous anger at Luc.

Luc knew he was playing dirty, but he moved his arm back just a bit, keeping his hand on the butt of his gun, knowing the move gave the *vicomte* a peek at the weapon. As minister of protocol, Luc was licensed to carry a gun. Even though he didn't relish the thought of shooting anyone, he was ready to protect the king he'd vowed to defend and serve.

The move had the desired effect. Yves's eyes flashed a barely perceptible start of surprise and he settled down, leaving the talking to his father.

For a man in his fifties, Yves was more child than adult with that hair-trigger temper, Luc thought. The only reason he'd gained a seat on the council was because Pascal was first cousin to the king and the king was Yves's godfather.

The nepotism was so deep that Luc was always afraid he would drown in it. It almost brought down his family when the Patrice scandal broke. Yet, in the end, the De Vaugirard strength had merely bent him. It did not break him.

They would never break him. And he would personally ensure that they didn't get the best of Sophie, either.

"Now that we all have our wits about us," said Pascal, "if I may point out something with all due respect, Your Majesty?"

The king sighed. "What?"

Pascal arched a brow, but remained as smooth and unmovable as a river stone. "Your Highness, one thing you must consider before you introduce your granddaughter to society is that Sophie is the daughter of your Sylvie, God rest her soul."

The *comte* crossed himself. The ostentatious show made

Luc want to spit. That man was no more a devout Catholic than the dog that begged for scraps at the kitchen door. And his grief for the late *princesse* was equally contrived. Luc had a sixth sense for this type of deceit, and his BS radar was buzzing.

"Yes, make your point, Pascal," the king snapped impatiently.

Sudden anger lit the *comte's* eyes, but disappeared as fast as it flashed. "The constitution clearly states that the heir to the throne must be of legitimate birth." His voice was not as patronizing as it had been a moment ago.

In fact, it held a slight edge. Luc did not like where this was going.

"The king and the Crown Council can change the constitution if they so choose." The words leaped out before he could stop them. Three pair of eyes pinned him to the spot.

King Bertrand smiled. "Yes, that is exactly what I intended."

"Ah, but I must remind you, to do that requires the unanimous agreement of the council," said Pascal.

"But of course," said the king as if it were a given.

"I dare say you will be shy at least two votes," said Yves. "Therefore a change will be impossible."

King Bertrand looked crushed.

"Why would you do that without even giving Princess Sophie a chance?" Luc spat out the words. "Because regardless of what the constitution says, she remains your *princesse.*"

"When did this become your business?" hissed Pascal.

"He does seem to have gotten awfully cozy with Madame Baldwin," said Yves. "In fact, if I didn't know better, I'd venture to say that it looks as if he were trying to further his own interests through the king's granddaughter."

The *vicomte* shrugged. "After all, social climbing does run in his family."

The king slammed both hands down on the table. "Get out, both of you. Get out *now!*"

As anger surged, something else clicked in Luc's gut. Something to the tune of the *vicomte doth protest too much.* It wasn't anything concrete—other than the assertions of social climbing and that it was a classic pot-and-kettle situation. The De Vaugirards were the first to *further their own interests.* Still, something in the exchange had set off the alarms…. It smacked of how those who have something to hide often make a stink about the very infraction of which they're guilty—like a man who is having an affair suddenly accusing his wife of flirting, to deflect his own guilt.

Luc did his best to separate personal dislike of the De Vaugirards so that he could be objective, but it was getting harder to find unbiased ground.

How much of the loathing he felt came from wanting to see his enemy taken down and how much was legitimate?

That answer remained to be seen.

However, two things were certain: He wouldn't stop until he could clearly answer that question; and until he did, he needed to distance himself from Sophie, for her own good.

She was the *princesse,* and when he was around her he tended to lose his head—to linger in thoughts of the sublime way she smelled, to stand much too near her, and give in to the temptation to touch her.

He would always be her loyal servant.

One who would never forget his place.

* * *

Sophie walked through the state dining room, feeling displaced, like a child in the way as the adults rushed around getting the place ready for a special occasion.

The table looked beautiful—set with the finest crystal, china and silver. The centerpiece with its harvest-colored flowers, wispy wheat stalks and mini pumpkins looked like something out of a *Better Homes and Gardens* editorial. And the smells of turkey, sage and spices made her stomach rumble.

It was the perfect Thanksgiving, and she didn't have to lift a finger. As nice as it sounded, it really did feel odd.

She and Frank were still together this time last year. It was their last holiday as a family. As usual, he had been no help. She'd worked the day before Thanksgiving, did the shopping on the fly the night before. He'd yelled because she'd paid too much for a fresh turkey since there wasn't enough time to thaw a frozen bird, complained that she should've been more organized like his mother used to be.

Then she dragged herself out of bed at four-thirty in the morning to begin preparing the dinner. By the time the three of them sat down to eat, Sophie was ready to fall asleep sitting up.

Her parents couldn't join them last year because her dad had been sick. At least they were together this year, even if she felt removed and everything was a little topsy-turvy—especially the way she anticipated spending the evening with Luc.

Something had shifted today. She had awakened this morning unsure whether duty or something more personal kept bringing him back. Yet after he'd walked her back to the apartment after the Crown Council meeting—after the way he'd touched her, almost possessively, in Marci's office; after the feel of his hand on her back and the way he'd looked at her made her feel both protected and vulnerable…vulnerable to opening herself to him—she sensed it was edging toward the personal.

And getting personal with Luc Lejardin suited her just fine.

Sophie walked into the living room so that she could greet him when he arrived. She couldn't recall a single moment in her life before now when she'd been at a loss for something to do. Usually it felt as if she were trying to cram ten pounds of life into a three-pound bag. She was constantly juggling and praying that she didn't drop one of the fragile balls. There was always an after-school activity for Savannah, clients' files to update, bills to pay, clothes to wash, dishes to scrub….

The list went on and on.

Too much to do, too little time.

And here she sat, the *princesse* of St. Michel, with nothing to do—except attend luncheons and dinners and go girly over a man. For someone who'd gotten on her nerves the way he initially did, he'd really become important to her. She hadn't wanted to like him at first, but never in her life was she so glad to be wrong.

Her maid, Adèle, entered the room holding a lone crystal champagne flute.

"Madame, I thought you might care for some champagne."

"How very nice of you, Adèle."

Sophie accepted the glass, feeling a little guilty drinking fine champagne, which seemed to flow like water in the *Palais de St. Michel*. If they had a moat around this place, it would probably be full of the stuff.

Adèle stood there, looking hesitant, as if she had a question.

"Is everything all right?" Sophie asked. *Do you have enough to eat? Does your family have shelter?* The woman looked clean, well and rested. But if not her, then who? Who was it that the fine people of St. Michel overlooked with their collective blind eye?

"Well, Madame, I was told that you didn't need my services past seven this evening? That I was to have the night off?"

The woman looked wary, as if someone were playing a joke on her.

Sophie nodded. "It's Thanksgiving, Adèle. You should be home with your family."

Her guarded look morphed into one of confusion.

"Madame, with all due respect, we don't celebrate Thanksgiving in St. Michel."

Sophie smiled. "I know, but as hard as you work, you could still use a night off. Don't forget to take the meal I had the kitchen staff package for you. Maybe just this once, you and your family could celebrate Thanksgiving, too. It never hurts to count your blessings."

The confusion faded into gratitude. "Oh, it is very kind of you to think of me. It just happens that it is my son's birthday and he will be so surprised when I get home."

Her son's birthday? And she was working?

"Happy birthday to him. How old is he?"

"Six years old."

"Well, then, he definitely needs his mother. You may leave now and you will receive full pay. Go celebrate."

Adèle hadn't been gone ten minutes when one of the footmen entered the room with a note on a silver tray.

"A message for you, Madame."

Sophie took the note off the tray, feeling like a character in a Jane Austen novel—well, if Jane Austen had written a book set in a castle off the coast of France.

She ran her hand over the cream-colored linen envelope admiring the fine quality of the stationery before she pulled out the note:

Dear Madame Baldwin,
Thank you for the dinner invitation. I deeply regret that I will not be able to attend.
I remain your humble servant,
Luc Lejardin

Chapter Ten

So much for edging toward the personal.

Two weeks had passed and Sophie hadn't seen even a shadow of Luc. She thought about calling him since he'd programmed his number into her cell phone and told her to use it.

A couple of times, she'd even gone so far as to hold the phone in her hand and contemplate pushing the speed-dial button he'd programmed to call his number, but she couldn't bring herself to do it.

Please, never hesitate to call me. I am at your service, he'd said that day he delivered the phones. *I remain your humble servant...*he'd written in the note excusing himself from dinner.

Well, then where was he?

Luc was a busy man. His mission to bring her to St. Michel

was complete. He was probably enmeshed in another assignment and didn't have time for her because he just wasn't interested.

It was just that she thought he was a friend…. He certainly was a bright spot in this strange turn of events. She understood that he had a job to do, that he wasn't hired for her amusement. But she missed him. Couldn't he spare a few minutes?

She should call him…just to say hi…

And she would've if she hadn't been so busy overseeing the Christmas decorating, attending etiquette lessons and fittings, and organizing a toy-drive for the underprivileged that the Comte De Vaugirard had so cavalierly brushed off at the Crown Council luncheon two weeks ago.

Even in the midst of the rush, she missed him.

Was that such a bad thing?

Sophie was thinking about that as she went to join her grandfather for tea. They'd been having short, informal get-togethers all week. Sophie was touched by the effort he was making to get to know her.

"Are the Christmas decorations in your quarters to your liking?" He sat in the wingback chair next to Sophie, a sterling pot of Earl Grey and a selection of cakes on a tiered tray between them. He seemed more relaxed than ever, which in turn allowed her to relax.

"They're beautiful," she said. "The apartment looks like a wonderland."

It truly did. In addition to the wreaths and garlands, there were three Christmas trees: a small one in the foyer adorned with nutcracker ornaments; a massive regal Fraser fir in the living room decorated in white and gold; and a more traditionally trimmed blue spruce in the dining room decked out in an eclectic mix of ornaments in various shapes, sizes and colors.

"It was amazing," Sophie marveled. "Adèle asked me how I wanted the house decorated and within two days it was done."

King Bertrand smiled. "I'm glad you're pleased. And the deportment lessons? Are they going well?"

"Yes, fine."

It was the cotillion lessons she'd never received as a child. All week, she and Savannah had been working with teams of French teachers, etiquette and public relations specialists whose task it was to make them *princesse* perfect and put just the right spin on why Princess Sophie had been hiding all these years.

Their identity was still top secret, of course. She had a feeling that once the professionals were finished with them, they wouldn't even recognize themselves.

She glanced around her grandfather's office, at the antiques and gilded finery. From what she'd seen, not a corner of the palace had been left undecorated. It was beautiful, but expensive and foreign and so contrary to the life she was used to. The investment the king was making in her and her daughter would make it harder to walk away at the end of three months. But she needed more of a sense of purpose than seasonal decorating and an endless stream of fittings to make a life here.

An elegant porcelain nativity scene displayed on the credenza caught her gaze.

God, I'm so confused. Please send me a sign that will help me make the right decision for my daughter and myself.

She wasn't a religious woman, but somehow the universal familiarity of the manger was comforting. A sign of hope that transcended all languages.

And speaking of hope, it was on the tip of her tongue to ask about Luc—if her grandmother had seen him; if so, what he had been up to—when Marci knocked and opened the door hesitantly.

"*Pardonnez-moi,* Your Majesty, but the Vicomte De Vaugirard is here to see you. He says it's urgent."

Sophie's heart sank. Not exactly the sign she'd hoped for. She set down her cup ready to make an exit at the first opportunity.

"Send him in, please," said the king. "And please bring us another cup in case the *vicomte* would care for some tea."

Marci bowed and disappeared.

A moment later De Vaugirard entered and bowed. "Your Majesty."

"Yves, come in. Have a seat." The king gestured to the sofa across from him and smiled broadly.

Tall and slight with a delicate air about him, De Vaugirard wasn't quite *effeminate,* but just up to the line. With his graying hair and expensive clothes, he was handsome in a well-heeled, aristocratic sort of way. If Sophie didn't know better, she would've never have guessed he and her grandfather had been at bitter odds since her arrival. Well, except for traces of the same I-smell-something-rank expression she'd spied on his face that first day.

Yves's gaze shifted to Sophie, then back to the king.

"Perhaps I should come back another time," said Yves, "when you're not busy."

"Nonsense, Sophie and I were just enjoying some tea. Join us."

As if on cue, Marci entered with a fresh cup and saucer. She poured some tea for the *vicomte*. "Cream, sugar or lemon, *monsieur?*"

Yves sighed as if the situation pained him, and said, "Plain will do."

He seated himself on the sofa across from Sophie and the king and accepted the cup that Marci offered him.

Is this guy for real?

He was probably in his early fifties, yet his affected mannerisms made him seem much older. He was like a caricature, Sophie decided. The poster boy of spoiled privilege forced to slum with someone he deemed far beneath him.

The king made small talk. With an air that hovered somewhere between bored and downright disgusted, Yves mostly ignored Sophie. It seemed as if her grandfather was grasping at straws when he said, "It's ironic that you dropped by when you did, Yves. I was planning to call upon you today for a favor. I was wondering if you would be so good as to show Sophie around St. Michel? Give her the grand tour. She has been cooped up inside since she got here, and I know she'd like to get out. Since you know the delicacy of the *situation* until she has been formally presented to the public, I know I can trust you to use the utmost discretion in public."

The following Monday, Sophie sat in the apartment study at a gorgeous Louis XIV desk working on details of the toy-drive, which was shaping up nicely. They were set to deliver three hundred wrapped gifts to the St. Michel Community Center on Christmas Eve. She jotted a note to herself to ask her grandfather to appeal to the De Vaugirards, one more time to help deliver the toys as a goodwill gesture. They and council member Norbert Guillou were the only three who refused to participate. Sophie could read between the lines. They also happened to be the three dissenting council members who were against her succeeding her grandfather. Couldn't they rise above petty political differences one day of the year? Especially when it involved children?

Adèle knocked on the door and announced that she had a visitor in the living room. Sophie's heartbeat upped its tempo.

Luc?

She ran her fingers through her hair and wished she could slip into her bedroom to reapply her lipstick, but because the study was off the living room, she couldn't.

When she stepped out to greet the visitor and saw Yves De Vaugirard waiting, her spirits took a nosedive and her guard went up like a wall of steel bars.

No. Not him.

When her grandfather had suggested that he give Sophie the grand tour, the sourpuss could do nothing more than grunt.

Why was it that the wealthy could act inappropriately and it was called eccentric? Seems like Yves could stand a deportment refresher. All the more reason to show him how it should be done.

"Vicomte De Vaugirard, to what do I owe this pleasure?" She didn't even sound like herself. She crossed the parquet floor and extended her hand, just like Daphne, her coach, had taught her, even though it felt awkward and insincere.

Yves bowed stiffly and straightened.

He made her feel uneasy the way he watched her with those small ice-blue eyes of his. They seemed to bore right through her. Did the guy not even blink?

"Thank you for receiving me without an appointment, Your Highness."

Your Highness?

Wait a minute. This from the guy who was so adamantly opposed to her very presence?

In the spirit of good manners, she decided to talk to him for a few moments and then feign an appointment.

"I hope you don't mind, but I took the liberty of checking your schedule with the king's secretary and since you had a free afternoon—"

Or not…

"I would be very honored if I might spend some time with you this afternoon," he said, "and show you the beauty of St. Michel as your grandfather suggested."

She must have looked utterly flummoxed because he added, "You are a matter of…great importance to our country. I would be remiss if I didn't make an effort to get to know you…personally."

What? Well…this was certainly an unexpected change of heart, but definitely a step in the right direction. Her grandfather would be so pleased.

"Please, have a seat." She gave him her best *princesse* smile, and started to order some coffee, but he interrupted.

"Excuse me, *Your Highness.*" He gave an affected bow of the head with the words. "If I may be so bold, I know a lovely place that overlooks the water where we might enjoy tapas and wine. It would be my honor if you will allow me the privilege of spending the afternoon with you."

A chance to leave the palace? After being cooped up inside for two weeks? The place was starting to feel like a prison.

Savannah was at school and would be occupied for the day.

Sophie was afraid her daughter would get behind in her studies and had insisted that her daughter go to a real school with kids her own age before they drove each other crazy. Under strict orders not to spill the *princesse's* beans, Savannah was enrolled in the best private school in the area.

Going with Yves was the perfect opportunity to do a little internal PR, a chance to win him over and prove that she wasn't simply the poor North Carolina hick he and his father had made her out to be.

Maybe it was the principle of the matter, but for some reason she was more determined than ever to make friends with Yves De Vaugirard.

This grand tour might be the perfect way to do it.

Her mind skittered back to the night she first arrived and how Luc, leaning into her, invading her space, had promised to show her the island. But where was he? He'd disappeared without so much as a goodbye.

"A tour and lunch would be wonderful," Sophie said, ignoring the disappointment that she would tour the island for the first time without Luc.

Fifteen minutes later, they were in Yves's car negotiating the serpentine turns and hills along the narrow coastal road that led away from the castle. Looking down the steep, rocky embankment into the sea below, Sophie grasped for conversation to distract herself from the mean case of vertigo that threatened each time she looked down.

"What kind of car is this?" she asked for lack of another neutral topic.

It was probably a gauche question—though Daphne hadn't specifically spelled out asking the brand of car to be among the many taboos to be avoided during polite St. Michelian conversation. Plus she'd never seen anything like the black and cherry two-seater. The way it slanted down in the back, swelled up in the middle, yielding to a curved nose, it looked almost reptilian.

To her relief Yves smiled warmly and purred, "A Bugatti Veyron. You like?"

She almost expected him to reach out and stroke the dash. "It's very nice."

The admiration of his *baby* seemed to break the ice. As they made their way down the rocky mountain that housed the palace, she was surprised by how warm and personable Yves proved to be. He pointed out various spots of interest and shared fascinating bits of trivia such as the stretch of road where a James Bond movie had been filmed.

Around the next bend, Yves abruptly pulled the car over onto the shoulder. For a panicked instant, Sophie feared they might slide off the road. She reached out for the dash to brace herself as Yves stopped the car. She slanted him an alarmed glance and thought she caught the barest trace of a smirk curving up his thin lips. Was he trying to scare her?

"What's wrong?" she asked. "Why are we stopping?"

His face was somber again. He rolled down the car windows, then stretched his right arm across the back of her seat and leaned in to point toward the passenger-side window with his left hand, nearly surrounding her with his body.

It gave her the creeps, especially when he turned his head and looked at her at such close range. His face was much too near; the mingled scent of his musky cologne and warm, stale breath nearly overwhelmed her.

There was nothing romantic in the gesture. The way he studied her was calculated, almost a bit passive aggressive.

"This is the unfortunate place where Princesse Celine lost control of her car and plunged to her death."

His words were matter-of-fact, devoid of emotion.

Sophie shuddered as a sudden cold chill swept over her. She turned away from Yves, moving closer to the window, gazing intently down the steep incline, more to escape him than to see the morbid site.

It was a gray day. The temperature had dropped probably ten degrees since she had arrived in St. Michel—since that night in the limo when Luc sat so close and she'd fought the overwhelming urge to move toward him. Not like this with Yves, who conjured up a strange mixture of sadness and unease.

She struggled with a ridiculous sense of loss but couldn't quite define it. The loss of Celine and Sylvie who'd died before their time? The fact that Luc had all but disappeared. It seemed inappropriate to even think about him right now.

Finally, after another clumsy moment, Yves shifted back into his seat. They rode silently until he steered the car into the valet parking line of a busy restaurant that fronted a rocky stretch of beach. She was tempted to ask him to take her back to the palace, but didn't want to chance offending him and worsening relations. After all, he really hadn't crossed the line of inappropriateness. Though he'd edged right up to it. Nothing Luc hadn't done. The only difference was, with Luc, she'd walked right up to that line with him and was just about to drag him over. Until he stopped calling.

She needed to stop thinking about Luc.

"I thought you might enjoy a light bite to eat and some champagne." Yves sat with his left elbow resting on the open window frame, his right wrist draped over the steering wheel, as blasé as if the awkwardness at the top of the hill had never happened.

A cold wind off the water blew in through the open windows, biting through Sophie's silk blouse. She rubbed her arms trying to warm herself.

"You are chilly?" Yves asked. "Allow me."

He unbuckled his seat belt, removed his navy blue wool sports coat, and leaned over to place it around Sophie's shoulders.

Sitting there in that expensive sports car, parked in front of the Côte d'Azur, the strangest thought washed over her: She'd come a long, long way from that hideous mustard-colored coat. Shouldn't that feel good, rather than so unsettling?

Ah, well....

She was just about to thank him for the nice gesture when he leaned in closer, and this time, she thought he actually might try to kiss her.

What the heck?

Panic seized her and she fought the urge to push him away. Instead, she turned her head to the right and pretended to brush something off the jacket's shoulder.

Was this what he was pathetically fumbling for up at the site of Celine's crash? Only now they were in public. In full view of the valets and people coming and going.

This was worse than any bad date she'd ever been on. And it wasn't even a date. It was a reconnaissance mission, a goodwill attempt to make peace with the enemy. All for her grandfather. For St. Michel...Because of that, if she didn't do something to allow him to save face, this little outing might end up doing more damage than good.

"Thank you, Yves." She wouldn't look at him, but she kept her voice light. "I really should've brought a jacket."

At that moment, thank God, the valet appeared at his door. Still playing the gentleman, Yves got out and walked around to the passenger side, helped Sophie out of the car and into an embrace, kissing full and deep.

Then it was as if everything moved in slow motion. One moment she was struggling to get out of Yves's arms, the next she was staring down the lens of a camera as a photographer documented the sordid exchange, then Luc and three *Men in Black* appeared from out of nowhere. As two of Luc's men shielded her from the fray, the other went after the photographer, while Luc whisked her to a waiting car, away from the press and the Vicomte de Vaugirard.

"What the hell were you doing with Yves De Vaugirard?" Luc spat the words as he slammed his Audi into fifth gear, unsure if he was more outraged at the *vicomte* for putting his hands on Sophie or mad at himself for leaving her alone with the snake.

"What was I *doing?*" She sounded just as angry as he felt. "I wasn't *doing* anything. My grandfather asked the *vicomte* to show me St. Michel. I have no idea why he kissed me like that. God knows I didn't lead him on."

Luc slanted a glance at her in time to see a rogue tear meander down her cheek as she scrubbed the back of her hand over her lips.

Thank God she'd followed protocol and informed the king's secretary where she was going. Marci had immediately phoned Luc. Something about it smelled funny. Following his instincts, Luc decided to tail De Vaugirard on this unlikely outing. And he was damn glad he did.

Now two of his men were in a separate car, making sure

no one followed Luc as he drove Sophie to safety. He was still awaiting word from Dupré as to whether he was successful in wrangling the camera away from the photographer.

Sophie was shaking. He wanted nothing more than to stop the car and hold her, but he couldn't. Even though he'd effectively ditched the media, it was only a matter of minutes before they caught up.

The last thing they needed was for the paparazzi to come upon Sophie and him parked along the side of the road.

But Luc had a better idea. He steered the car off the highway and onto a back road.

"Where are you going?" Sophie asked swiping at a tear.

"I live about a half-mile from here. I'm taking you to my house so that you can compose yourself before we go back to the castle."

He made a right turn, then a quick left and his phone rang. "Did you catch him?" he barked.

"The photographer handed off the camera to a waiting car," said Dupré. "This looked like a pretty tight operation. Someone tipped them off. I wonder who they're working for?"

Luc growled under his breath. "Yeah, I wonder."

He snapped the phone shut.

The minute Yves had Sophie in his arms, the scumbag paparazzo swooped in, got the shots and threw the camera to the driver, who took off in the car while the photographer took off on foot.

The plan had worked too damn perfectly. And it smacked of De Vaugirard.

The photos discrediting the newfound heir to the throne were sure to run in the paper the next day.

But what the De Vaugirards didn't realize was that in their desperation, they were getting sloppy. They were tipping their hand and it was just a matter of time before Luc had the concrete evidence he needed to nail them.

This war had been a long time coming—vengeance for his father's death and the king's lost family. For his friend Antoine.

It was a war Luc was hell-bent on winning.

"What the heck just happened back there, Luc?"

"I hate to tell you this, but you were set up."

"Set up? What do you mean?"

Luc glanced in his rearview mirror to make sure they hadn't been followed before he pressed a button that opened the wrought-iron gates surrounding his house.

"Since news of the *vicomte* hitting the town with yet another woman is hardly fodder for the paparazzi, I'm afraid that possibly someone has leaked your story," he said as the gates closed behind them. "Tomorrow it is likely that all of St. Michel will know about its new heiress."

"Oh, my God." She pressed her hands over her beautiful mouth.

Luc drove into the garage, closing the door so that it might serve as a second layer of privacy and protection.

"Can't you stop them?" she asked. "I mean, come on, my grandfather is the *king.* Doesn't he have any power?"

Luc opened the car door. "Unfortunately, not over the press. Especially when they're working for the De Vaugirards."

The car's engine ticked in the quiet garage.

"They sound like mafia," she said.

He opened the car door. "Let me assure you, the mafia has nothing on the *comte.*"

Luc turned off the security system and held the door for her, fighting the urge to pull her into his arms and promise he would do everything in his power to protect her. Even after two weeks of keeping his distance, the woman still affected him. What in the world was he going to do?

They entered the kitchen, which opened onto a large living room that had a breathtaking view of the sea.

As Luc removed his shoulder holster and set it on the kitchen counter, Sophie moved, transfixed, into the living room and stared out the large plateglass windows.

Luc drew some water in a kettle and put it on to boil.

"How can he get away with this?" she murmured, her back still to him as she gazed out at the ocean. "Better question is, why would he do this? He has to know how much it will hurt my grandfather. Why would an old friend fight so vehemently against another over something that should be a celebration? My grandfather thought every member of his family was dead, but he still has me. Shouldn't his *oldest friend* be happy for him?"

The look on her face was heartbreaking. She moistened her lips, and the simple action reminded him that even though he'd removed himself from temptation, even distance couldn't tame his craving for her.

"One would think," he murmured.

Luc had his theories, but he couldn't tell her. Not until he was absolutely certain. In the meantime, it was imperative that she and Savannah not be left unattended. He couldn't take that chance.

Luc walked up behind her with a small cashmere throw and draped it around her, resisting the urge to run his hands down her arms and taste the ivory skin where her neck met her shoulders.

"Did he hurt you?"

She shook her head and turned to face him as she pulled the blanket tighter. "Only my pride. I feel like such an idiot. I actually thought I was making headway by going with him today. I should've known better."

She looked up at him with fresh tears glimmering in her eyes.

"No," he said. "There was no way to know without someone warning you about him. I should never have left you alone."

She bit her lip. He saw her throat work, and his heart turned over in response.

"Luc, where have you been?" Her voice was barely a whisper. "I've missed you."

His mouth went dry. As he searched for the words, she reached out and ran a gentle finger along his jawline.

His head tilted into her touch and his arms went around her, gently pulling her close. He wanted to keep her here. Safe and away from barracudas like de Vaugirard. Her mouth was just a breath from his. Those lips…so tempting…would taste so sweet. A rush of desire urged him to give in, to sample the taste and feel of her while the rest of the world melted away. There were so many reasons he shouldn't…but at the moment, he couldn't seem to remember any of them—

The teakettle whistled, sounding an alarm, warning him to back away.

"I need to get that." He stepped back, away from her touch, away from temptation as reality rushed in and common sense chastised him.

The *princesse* was vulnerable after her ordeal with the *vicomte*. How could he even think the things he had contemplated?

"Let's have some coffee and then we need to get you back to the castle and begin damage control."

When Sophie and Luc returned to the castle, he took Sophie back to her apartment to freshen up. He needed to clear his head and focus on the De Vaugirard situation before he went to the king's chambers. After giving the situation some thought, Luc decided it was his duty to share his theory—though unfounded—with the king. So much of his job revolved around gut instinct. The big problem was if he waited to test these theories, by the time he had solid proof, sometimes it was too late. In the wake of what happened with Antoine and his family, he couldn't afford to chance waiting.

When Luc told the king of Yves's very odd and very public display of affection and the ensuing photography, King Bertrand was furious and visibly shaken.

"It makes no sense," King Bertrand insisted. "The paparazzi are always milling about down by the water. It had to be a fluke, a case of Yves being in the wrong place at the wrong time."

"Unless," Luc asserted, "Yves intended for the incident to be photographed."

The king's eyes flashed.

"Absolutely not. Why would he do that? He knows better than anyone what a disaster it would be for word to get out before we're ready to present Sophie."

"Exactly," Luc said. "What I am about to suggest will not be easy for you to hear, Your Majesty, but it is my duty as minister of protocol to alert you to potential problems. Since the loss of the prince and his family, I must remind you that the Vicomte De Vaugirard's name has been mentioned as a likely successor."

He paused to give the king a chance to digest what he was suggesting. But the man simply stared back at him with uncomprehending bewilderment.

"Your Majesty, you upset the plan by adding your long-lost granddaughter into the equation just when the *vicomte* thought he was home free. Can you think of a better way for him to discredit Sophie than by marring her introduction to the people of St. Michel?"

The king's mouth fell open. Then he found his words. "Watch what you're saying, Lejardin. This is my *godson* you are defaming. The son of my lifelong friend. You seem to forget he would have been putting his own reputation on the line if he'd staged a setup with these photographs."

"Your Majesty, I humbly beg your pardon, but the *vicomte* has delighted in building just that sort of reputation. He thrives on that type of publicity. So much so that the *vicomte* out with a new woman ceases to be news. Unless the press had been tipped off that his latest conquest wasn't just any woman."

The king flinched.

"Do not be crass, Monsieur Lejardin."

He expected this reaction and knew it wasn't easy for the king to hear.

"I humbly beg your pardon, I hate having to bring you this news. But this was a very well choreographed operation. One of my men went after the photographer to try to retrieve the camera, but there was a getaway car waiting. The media had been tipped off and I will work to find out who informed them."

The look of doubt that washed over the king was heart-breaking. This was the part of Luc's job he hated the most—exposing lies, shattering trust. Yet it was either that or expose the king and his family to unnecessary risk. Too much death had already happened under his command. His heart ached at the thought of Antoine, whose memory was already seeming to dim in the month he'd been gone.

There had already been too many innocent lives lost. There would be no more. Especially not Sophie. He couldn't fathom the thought of losing her and, if forced, he would fight to the death to protect her.

"With whom have you shared your theory?" the king asked.

"No one else, Your Majesty. It is much too sensitive a matter to carelessly bandy about."

The king stroked his beard and nodded, a faraway look in his eyes.

"However," Luc continued, "given the circumstances, it is my duty to inform you of any potential threats. To that end, I have heightened security measures concerning Princess Sophie and Princess Savannah. If there is need for them to leave the palace, I will personally escort them. It is also prudent for you to use the utmost caution as you go about your business, Your Majesty."

"You make it sound as if we are preparing for an imminent attack."

The older man looked weary, as if all the fight had been zapped out of him. Although Luc was betting against himself by hoping he was wrong, the alternative was unthinkable.

"Your Majesty, I hope to God we aren't. However, we can't take any chances."

The intercom interrupted them. Marci announced Sophie, the Vicomte De Vaugirard, and Pierre Benzanet, the chief of palace communications, who had been summoned to formulate a crisis PR plan that would somehow turn this mess in their favor.

It seemed that everyone was arriving at once. Luc was curious to see how De Vaugirard would treat Sophie now that they were holding in the eye of the storm.

The *vicomte* was a good actor. He feigned concern for Sophie, he even manages a bit of stiff praise for Luc for miraculously being in the right place at the right time.

"Lejardin, it seems you are everywhere these days."

Luc couldn't put his finger on it, but something was off. Maybe it was the way Yves chose to perch on the wingback chair rather than claiming the empty space on the couch next to Sophie, as Luc longed to do.

In fact, when Luc did just that, De Vaugirard didn't seem to notice. There wasn't an ounce of territorial concern or other indication of the attraction that might inspire a man to spontaneously pull a woman into a passionate, very public kiss. No, every ounce of Yves's focus was trained upon Benzanet.

"The press office phone will ring nonstop once the paper is released," said the communications chief. "The media will surely demand an audience with Princesse Sophie and the *vicomte*. It is imperative that we agree on a plan for a morning press conference before we leave this office tonight. Because the obvious question on everyone's mind will be, who is Sophie Baldwin and what exactly is the nature of her relationship with the Vicomte De Vaugirard?"

Chapter Eleven

*R*elationship with the Vicomte De Vaugirard?

The thought and ensuing mental flash of what a relationship with Yves would entail made Sophie feel vaguely ill.

There was no way.

Absolutely no way she could even pretend to play the part when she didn't feel that way about him. Because when she was in love it consumed her, it radiated from the inside out like a light she had no intention of veiling.

Reflexively she glanced at Luc. As if he sensed her, his gazed flicked to her and a knowing look passed between them. The single glance said that he, too, thought this was a crock of PR crap. A private conversation between them in the midst of a crowded room.

That alone made Sophie feel better.

Benzanet excused himself to get to work on the crisis PR

plan, after suggesting that they go with the idea of a brief and very innocent *relationship* between the *princesse* and the *vicomte*. The two could amicably "part ways" over the next few days. They could be seen out to dinner together, perhaps be photographed out for a cruise on the *vicomte's* yacht. Given the *vicomte's* social standing, it might even be a good way to introduce her. A sophisticated royal romance was always a surefire way to raise the monarchy's approval rating.

If Sophie felt vaguely ill before, now she was downright queasy.

After the door shut, the *vicomte* sighed. "Well, this is quite a little mess we've gotten ourselves into, isn't it, now?"

We? He made it sound as if they'd sneaked off together for an afternoon tryst. The only *we* she could come up with was that that must have been a mouse she felt in his pocket when he pulled her into that sloppy kiss.

"If only I had known I was putting her at risk," Yves said to the king, "I would have never heeded *your* suggestion and gone through with the outing."

Oh, so now it was the king's fault for suggesting the outing. The vicomte *certainly didn't like to take responsibility, did he?*

Yves looked nonplussed and much too effeminate as he crossed his right leg over his left knee. He seemed to be avoiding looking at Sophie. But as he pursed his little mouth, the expression made Sophie remember how he'd pecked at her with those thin lips and an angry bubble burst inside her.

"Why did you kiss me?" She hadn't meant to say the words aloud. They just sort of popped out like an errant hiccup.

At least the *vicomte* had the decency to look embarrassed. He studied his shoes. Then his gaze slanted toward the king and back to the floor before he cleared his throat.

Still not looking at her.

"*Pardonnez-moi,* Your Highness. I couldn't seem to help myself." He gave an awkward little shrug.

What...?

She should've been flattered that she'd inspired so much passion in a man that he'd be so moved as to lose control of his wits and lay a big passionate kiss on her in public...but *puh-lease.* Did he really expect her to believe he was so overcome by passion that he *couldn't seem to help himself.*

There was one important element missing from the equation—passion.

So...why did he do it?

"I assure you, madame, I meant no harm." The *vicomte* lifted his chin regally. "And I would very much like to see you again."

Sophie wanted to squirm. Or maybe laugh. She wanted to call him on this contrived, robotic request for a second date and ask him *why?* She wasn't buying it.... Was anyone else? She glanced at Luc and her grandfather. They both wore poker faces, but something in Luc's eyes told her to be quiet. To wait and talk to him.

That he had the answers she was looking for.

"Well," said the king, "I suggest we call it a night. It's best that we get some rest before tomorrow's press conference."

With a hasty bow to the king, the *vicomte* mumbled pleasantries to Sophie and Luc and made his retreat.

Right. He was so eager to see me again he didn't even offer to walk me home.

Thank God. Because she didn't know what she would've done if he tried to kiss her again. This time when no one was looking. Imagine that.

In the awkward moment before she left, she tried to somehow reassure her grandfather that everything would be okay…but the words escaped her. All she could say was, "I'm sorry."

All he could offer was a weary smile and a valiant "I'm sure everything will be fine. Get your rest, because tomorrow will be a trying day."

By the time Sophie and Luc left, the corridor was eerily silent except for the echoing cadence of their shoes on the marble floor.

With every step the echo seemed to sing: *mistake, mistake, mistake, mistake.*

Coming to St. Michel was a mistake of colossal proportions.

"What was I thinking?" she murmured.

"I don't know," Luc said. "Tell me what you're thinking."

Sophie shook her head. "Maybe the Crown Council's right? Maybe it's time for a new era? Because I'm certainly in way over my head."

"So you are saying that you're better suited for gray cubicles and endless stacks of case files?"

"At least in my job with the county, I knew what I was doing. It was something worthwhile. I was helping people rather than destroying a dynasty."

Her heart grew heavy with memories of Laura. She hoped her boys were doing okay after losing their mother, wished there was something more she could do for them, but she was so far away.

"I can tell you that as the heiress to the throne of St. Michel, you will have many opportunities to make a difference. As the *princesse,* you have carte blanche. The only way you will bring down the Founteneau dynasty is if you quit. You don't strike me as a quitter, Sophie."

Oh. Well, thanks. I think.

How did he do that? How was it that he had that uncanny ability to disarm her? To make her feel as if anything was possible. Anything in the world…especially between them.

They walked side by side, neither of them speaking again until they reached the front door of Sophie's apartment.

Claude met them in the entryway with a polite bow. "*Bonsoir,* Madame Baldwin, Monsieur Lejardin. I trust you had a good day?"

Oh, if he only knew.

"It was fine, thank you, Claude. And you?"

The butler looked a bit taken aback by the question, as if he weren't used to people asking. "Yes, madame, it was a quiet day. When would you care for your dinner and will Monsieur Lejardin join you?"

"Please stay, Luc," she said. "I could use the moral support when I prepare Savannah for tomorrow." She dreaded the thought, but she had to do it. Before Savannah saw a picture of her mother kissing the *vicomte* plastered all over the paper. Worse yet, she had no idea the angle the paper would take with the story or what they'd say. Savannah needed to be prepared. And so did her parents. The task almost overwhelmed her.

Until Luc said, "Of course. I'd love to."

The way Luc looked at her made Sophie's stomach roll over. To pry her thoughts loose from the pull of his dark, enigmatic gaze, she said, "And Claude, speaking of Savannah, where is she?"

The clock in the hall showed it was after seven. Sophie was surprised her daughter hadn't already called looking for her.

"Mademoiselle Savannah asked a school friend to stay for dinner. They have already eaten and are in her room doing homework."

Homework? Without my having to threaten to ground her? At least something went right today.

Savannah had been talking about the friends she'd made in school. For the first time since the divorce, her daughter actually seemed happy. Sophie's heart weighed heavy with the thought that one news story might change that.

"I guess it will just be the two of us for dinner. Please let us know when it's ready."

The butler gave a little bow. *"Très bien, madame."*

"Thank you, Claude."

As Sophie led Luc into the living room she suddenly became aware that they were alone. Aside from the few staff who remained after hours, Savannah and her friend, it was just them. No cameras, no *vicomte*. It was an enemy-free zone. It felt safe to be tucked away with Luc, insulated from the real world.

It was hard to believe that not even a month ago he had been a stranger delivering a message that totally changed her world. Now it seemed as if he was one of the only people in the world—or at least in this strange world of St. Michel— whom she could trust. One of the only people in the world she wanted to spend time with. Balm for her weary soul.

There was a fire in the fireplace. That and the glow from the Christmas tree was the only lighting in the room. If her heart hadn't been so weighed down by the baggage of today's fiasco, it might have seemed romantic.

She was beginning to feel like the queen of bad timing.

"Have a seat, I'm going to tell Savannah I'm back."

As she walked out of the room, she wished she could go

back and undo the moment she'd agreed to go out with the Vicomte De Vaugirard. But this was not a fairy tale where she could look into a magic mirror and wish away the bad. Oh no, this mess was her introduction to the people of St. Michel and the only thing she could do was deal with it, and pray that somehow she could turn it around in her favor. As if.

She could hear laughter when she reached her daughter's door. It was like music to hear Savannah so happy, and Sophie stood there for a moment savoring the sound. When she knocked on the door, Savannah called "Come in." Sophie opened the door and saw Savannah and her friend lying on their stomachs on the Persian carpet in front of the fireplace. Their books were open and they were sharing a bowl of popcorn. They seemed to be having the time of their lives— as fourteen-year-olds should. The girl wasn't pierced (beyond the ears) or tattooed (that she could see…*nah,* not on this one). She didn't even know her name, but she could tell the girl wasn't the type.

They were just two teenagers having fun—*doing their homework.*

"Mom! Hi, this is my friend Camille." She said the name with the proper French inflection—*Ca-mee*—and the girls giggled again. "Camille, this is my mom."

She smiled and greeted Sophie politely. And she didn't even have a sullen, pierced pout. How refreshing.

"I invited her to stay for dinner, I didn't think you'd mind," Savannah said. "Can she sleep over?"

Oh, how Sophie wished she could say yes. But she couldn't.

"Nice to meet you, Camille. You two certainly sound like you're having fun. How about a sleepover this weekend, okay?"

Collectively the girls groaned, "No, tonight!" But it wasn't the typical *battle call* that usually followed Sophie's shooting down one of Savannah's spur-of-the-moment ideas. Seconds later they were giggling again.

"I'm having dinner with Luc. But just holler if you all need anything."

They were too busy making plans for Friday night to hear her. But that was okay. That was the way it should be. Savannah happy and laughing, having fun doing the things that normal fourteen-year-olds do.

As Sophie stood outside Savannah's closed door, the strangest feeling washed over her. Yes, *this* was the way it *should* be. She didn't want to take this away from her daughter. This was her birthright. Hers, too. Was she going to let a greedy *vicomte* rob them of it?

A strange, shaky feeling washed over her. Like an adrenalin rush. Akin to what it must be like to contemplate jumping out of an airplane. Something she would never do. But sometimes you have to step out of your comfort zone to really find yourself.

Taking chances was exactly what she was thinking about when she stepped back into the living room and saw Luc sitting on the couch in the half-light of the fire, holding a flute of champagne. He stood when she entered the room.

"Claude thought we might like an aperitif." Luc lifted the other crystal glass off the coffee table and held it out to her. She took it and scooted a little closer to him on the couch. And he didn't seem to mind. They clinked glasses and sipped the golden liquid.

"Savannah's having such a good time with her friend. She seems so happy here. That alone could convince me to stay."

Luc smiled. "Well, then, I shall do everything in my power to ensure that your daughter remains in a constant state of bliss."

He reached out and toyed with a lock of Sophie's hair. There was something intimate about the gesture and she shifted closer to him. The fire warmed the room—or maybe it was the unspoken that lingered between them. Words that needed to be said.

"Have you been avoiding me?" The words escaped in a rush, before she had the good sense to think about what she was asking.

He let her hair fall, sipped his drink as if thoughtfully searching for what he wanted to say.

"Because if you have been staying away on purpose, I think you should know there hasn't been a day that's gone by that I didn't long to see you."

Then he simply nodded.

She squeezed her eyes shut. "Why, Luc? Why have you been avoiding me?"

He exhaled, and the breath sounded heavy and jagged, full of the same longing that was about to make her burst. The way he looked at her was devastating.

"Because of wanting to do this," he murmured as he ran his thumb slowly over her bottom lip. "And this." He softly traced the plane of her cheek. "And this." His hands were in her hair now, pulling her toward him.

It wasn't the first time she'd wondered what he'd taste like. No, that question had bloomed the very moment he'd appeared at her front door that very first day. The longing had never subsided. It lurked in the back of her mind as strongly as he'd stood by her—just as he was doing now—being her friend, her protector, her rock.

And then those lips she'd been dying to taste closed over hers, finishing what had almost begun at his house earlier that day. His kiss was surprisingly gentle. He tasted her, but didn't take her. He was so tender, tasting like a hint of champagne and something else, something uniquely Luc. As her lips opened under his, passion overtook her and for just a moment she wanted him to take her—right here, right now—in a hard, punishing kiss that would block out all the ugliness of the day…. He was nothing like Yves. He was the man she wanted to kiss…but Savannah could walk in…and Claude was due to call them to dinner any moment…and tomorrow the photo of her and Yves would be plastered all over town—

Breathless, she pulled away.

Luc blinked, looking a little dazed. "I'm sorry," he said. "I shouldn't have—I should go."

He stood, but she grabbed his hand.

"No, Luc. Please don't go. That was…" She searched his eyes as he stared down at her, uncertainty clouding his face. "That was wonderful, and something I've wanted for a long time. It's just that I can't masquerade as the girlfriend of one man when I'm involved with another."

God, one kiss didn't mean they were involved. But she didn't want this to end with one kiss. There was a lot more she wanted to explore with him. But first—

"I need to tell my grandfather in no uncertain terms that I won't pretend to be involved with Yves. I don't care if it is the easy way out."

Luc's expression shifted. When he sat back down, Sophie moved her hand from his arm to his hand.

"It was Yves's scheme that landed us in this position. As far as I'm concerned, he can lie in the bed he's made." She knew she was rambling, but she couldn't stop. "The only thing I will tell the press is I have no idea why he kissed me. If he goes off about how he *couldn't help* himself, he'll have to deal with my saying I do not return his feelings. I know it's harsh, but I know he's not telling the truth. He set me up to look like an idiot in front of the entire nation of St. Michel, so he's going to get himself out of the mess."

Sophie wanted to memorize the look on Luc's face. It was something between awe and admiration. There wasn't a hint of fear in reaction to the suggestion they might be "involved." No one had ever looked at her that way and it made her giddy…then breathless as she leaned in to taste his lips one more time.

"The king needs to know how I feel," she said, their lips a whisper apart.

As they sat there forehead to forehead, he gently stroked her cheek. "I think it is very important that your grandfather know how you feel. I would like to tell him that I feel very passionate about…you…doing what you feel is right. May I come with you to talk to him?"

Chapter Twelve

The cat was out of the bag.

She didn't even have to see the newspaper to know. It was evident in the reverent way the staff bowed when Sophie walked into the room. The former "Madame Baldwin" address was replaced with respectful murmurings of "Your Highness."

They knew.

Dressed in yet another Chanel suit that had appeared in her closet compliments of the couture fairy, Sophie resisted the urge to explain, because she hadn't talked to her grandfather this morning.

Last night, he flinched at Sophie wanting to deny any feelings for the *vicomte*. He wasn't convinced that leaving Yves to explain his actions to the media was the best way out of this.

"It will make it appear that there is infighting among the

Crown Council," he said. "It is imperative that we present a united front on all counts, especially since we will be digging ourselves out of the hole trying to explain why we hid you away all these years."

"What was wrong with the truth?" she'd asked.

He looked sad as he tried to explain, "Sometimes when it comes to matters of state, the truth isn't always as clear cut as one might like it to be."

That sounded like a load of political hogwash. She hated to level an ultimatum, but if being the heir to the throne and ultimately the queen of St. Michel meant compromising her integrity, meant pretending to be interested in a man like the Vicomte De Vaugirard…well then, she'd be on a plane back to Trevard quicker than Yves would have a new woman on his arm.

Luc stood by her the entire way, his professional opinion as minister of protocol and as a close personal friend never wavered under the political guilt trip her grandfather kept heaping on them.

The king finally agreed to discuss the situation with Pierre Benzanet so that he could factor it into his recommendations. They would meet early tomorrow morning before the scheduled pre-press conference briefing.

So, with everything pending, Sophie thought it best to resist explaining herself to the staff until after the briefing. Especially because she hadn't yet seen the paper.

As Sophie sat at her dressing table, a knock sounded on the bedroom door.

"Come in," she said, finishing the final stroke of mascara.

Adèle opened the door. "*Pardonnez-moi,* Your Highness." She curtsied. "I thought you might like some coffee and toast as you get ready this morning?"

"That's very nice of you, Adèle. Thank you."

The maid wheeled in a cart with a covered plate, a china cup and saucer, and a silver coffee pot. She poured the coffee, stirring in the perfect amount of cream, exactly the way Sophie liked it.

"Here you are." She set the cup and a plate of wheat toast on the left side of the dressing table.

"Thank you, Adèle. I appreciate your bringing this to me. I won't have time for breakfast this morning."

The maid made a polite bow and offered a shy smile as she pushed the cart toward the door. Sophie watched in the mirror as the woman paused in the threshold, turning back as if she wanted to say something.

"Your Highness?" she said hesitantly.

Sophie swiveled around on the round vanity stool to face her. "Yes?"

"Forgive me for being so bold." The maid wrung her hands. Sophie hoped she wouldn't ask questions, but if she did, she'd do her best to answer them honestly. That's all she could do.

"My *maman* had the great privilege of serving the Princesse Sylvie, God rest her soul." Adèle cast her eyes heavenward and crossed herself. "It is an honor and a privilege to have the opportunity to carry on that tradition by serving you."

The maid bobbed a quick curtsy and turned back to her cart.

Her mother knew Sylvie—my mother?

"Oh, Adèle, really? Does your mother still live in St. Michel?"

With hopeful eyes, Adèle turned back, nodding vigorously. "I have told her about you—how kind you are. Even before we knew you were—" Again, she gave a slight reverent bow and bit her lip as if remembering her place. "*Pardonnez-moi,* but you have always been so very kind, and I speak for the entire staff and many others when I say we believe you will serve St. Michel well."

Oh—the unexpected show of support stole Sophie's breath.

The maid bowed her head again and turned to go.

What a very sweet thing to say…

"Adèle, I would love to have tea with you and your mother. If you would care to and she would agree to come? I would love to ask her about my…my mother."

The maid gasped and her face lit up. "Oh, *mon Dieu,* yes, Your Highness." She curtsied again. "It would be the highest honor. We shall come whenever you summon us."

She knew my mother….

Of course Sophie had to wait to see what the press conference brought before she could extend an invitation to tea. Even so, her breath caught again. This was someone who *knew* Sylvie, someone who might be able to shed some light on the real person….

"Adèle, what is your mother's name?"

"Her name is Marie, Your Highness."

"Well, please tell Marie I look forward to meeting her soon."

Soon Luc arrived with a rolled copy of the *St. Michel Report* and the day took off as if she'd stepped on a roller skate.

"How bad is it?" she asked, knowing the answer from his solemn expression.

As he handed her the paper, she searched his eyes for traces of regret after last night. The news story should be the only thing on her mind right now, but Luc mattered. Besides her grandfather, he was her only political ally—not just that, he was more…. She couldn't imagine staying in St. Michel without him.

Luc met her gaze unflinchingly, and she gleaned silent reassurance from the way he looked her in the eyes.

Slowly, she unrolled the paper, her stomach churning as she did. The headline above the fold read: "The Secret Royal Heiress—King Bertrand kept Princesse Sylvie's illegitimate daughter a secret."

The story below the fold questioned: "St. Michel's Future Ruling Royals?" It speculated that Sophie might *marry* Yves as a way to get around the issue of her illegitimacy. That perhaps marriage to the king's likely successor was the only way the conservative Crown Council would acknowledge her as the heiress to the throne.

"Nice." If Yves De Vaugirard would've been near she would've boxed his ears.

The photos that accompanied the *Report's* exposé made it look as if the two had been making out all over town. Not only did it feature a photo of the lip lock in front of the restaurant—with a caption asking if Sophie was a wild child, following in the footsteps of Princesse Sylvie—but also shots of Yves and Sophie stopped at the site of Celine's accident; the way Yves had leaned in created the perfect angle for the editors to retouch the photos to look as though the two were kissing. The same for when he had leaned over her with his jacket as they waited for the valet at the restaurant—another contrived smooch shot.

Lovely. Just lovely. She wanted to scream. She wanted to tear the paper into shreds.

"Well, I think this is all the proof that we need that the *vicomte* set me up. Nobody can be in that many *wrong places* at the wrong time. Let's go talk to my grandfather. Now. Because there is no way I am going along with this so he can save face."

Luc didn't blame Sophie one bit for being angry. Frankly he wanted to deck the son of a bitch. He was just as eager as she was to talk to the king, to get a jump on figuring out how they were going to make De Vaugirard confess. *Yeah, right. As if the* vicomte *would do that.*

Still, if Sophie threatened to tell the press that the *vicomte's* kiss was both unexpected and *err,* that under no circumstance were they a couple, De Vaugirard would be forced into the uncomfortable corner of being publicly scorned by a suitor. This would be a new role for him given the legions of women who would give away their firstborn to date the man, who was billed as the king's likely successor.

Luc got a perverse thrill from the possibility of the *vicomte* being publicly humiliated.

It served him right for underestimating Sophie.

Luc and Sophie arrived at the king's chambers a full forty-five minutes before the scheduled briefing. They stepped inside the antechamber only to discover they were alone. Marci wasn't there.

Despite all that lay ahead of them, it was nice to have a moment alone together to catch their breath.

Sophie looked nervous. He hated what this was doing to her. Hated that Yves had snared her in his sticky web of self-importance. He'd walk on hot coals if that meant he could somehow make this situation go away. He reached out and ran a finger along her jaw.

He wanted to take her in his arms, but this wasn't the time or the place. Not when they were preparing to go to do internal battle over a kiss. The last thing they needed was another publicized display of affection. Even if this one was the real thing.

His hands claimed hers. He gave them a reassuring squeeze. "Everything is going to be all right. Don't forget that, okay?"

Sophie smiled and squeezed his hands in return.

Then suddenly the sound of an angry voice alerted them that someone was in the king's chambers—

"Need I remind you that we *must* secure a viable successor to ensure a smooth transition when the day comes that you are no longer 'leading' our country?"

The door leading from the antechamber into the king's office was cracked. Immediately, Luc's antenna signaled high alert.

It was Pascal De Vaugirard's voice. Luc held his index finger up to his lips. Sophie nodded her understanding.

The king's response was too low to hear what he was saying. Luc walked over to the door to better assess the situation.

"Once you are dead, the council will get its majority vote by default," the *comte* said. "Yves's ascent to power *will* happen. You can either graciously agree or die appearing to not have your country's best interest at heart."

He slowly eased open the door a fraction, just enough to allow him to peer inside without being seen.

He discovered that he and Sophie weren't the only ones who had planned an early meeting with the king. It seemed that Pascal and Yves De Vaugirard had the same idea.

King Bertrand didn't seem to be in immediate danger, so Luc kept his secret watch. A moment later he was glad he'd remained in the shadows because Yves De Vaugirard all but handed him the next piece of evidence he needed when he said, "If I were you, I'd take the proposal to heart. Or you just might find that we will get that majority vote sooner than you'd care to imagine, Your Majesty."

Luc pushed open the door. "Was that a threat, *vicomte?*"

All three turned to gape at him.

King Bertrand looked positively ashen, too stunned to speak. Arresting De Vaugirard was certainly one way to prevent him from putting his hands on Sophie. Luc was itching for a reason to put the conniving weasel away where he wouldn't cause any more harm.

"I beg your pardon, this is a private meeting," said Pascal. "You seem to make a habit of barging in where you don't belong."

Yves glared at Luc with a look that echoed his father's contempt.

"It is my duty to protect the king, and I am not comfortable with the threat I heard you issue." He kept his voice steady and low, putting his hand on his hip so that his jacket opened the slightest bit, exposing his holstered gun.

The king finally found his voice. "I'm sure you misunderstood the *vicomte,* Monsieur Lejardin. Yves is like a son to me and he would never endeavor to threaten me. Isn't that right, Yves?" He looked pointedly at the younger De Vaugirard, who did not answer. "Come, let us all begin again so that we may present a united front at the press conference."

* * *

It was no wonder that Pierre Benzanet was the chief of palace communications. He was a genius.

His plan for cleaning up the Yves scandal was to pin the onus on the *St. Michel Report*. The statement he penned claimed that the tabloid newspaper misrepresented the situation by manipulating the photos.

It wasn't a total lie—they had doctored two of the three to make it look as if Yves and Sophie had been hot and heavy all over town. The third? Well, even though it would've been more to Sophie's liking if Yves had faced public rejection—because he wouldn't admit he'd set her up for a humiliating introduction to the good people of St. Michel—this way everyone saved face. Plus if she was looking for a silver lining, the press conference gave Sophie a chance to plug her Christmas Eve toy-drive, broadening the scope from corporate and palace donations to pleas for public contributions.

Of course in between the photo controversy and the toy-drive announcement, there was the simple matter of where Princesse Sophie had been hiding all these years.

This was the crowning jewel, one for which Sophie could excuse the slight stretching of the truth with the photos. Because her grandfather told the truth.

In response to the question, he said, plain and simple, that upon learning of unwed Princesse Sylvie's pregnancy, he sent his newborn granddaughter to be raised in the United States because he thought he was giving her a better life rather than being raised with the stigma of being illegitimate.

"Hindsight is always clear," he said. "If I had the chance to go back and do it over again, I probably would have done some things differently—such as having contact with her as she was growing up. But she is here now, my heir when we thought the House of Founteneau had reached an end. A bright spot to light the darkness. I ask that you forgive my all-too-human mistakes, as Princesse Sophie has found it in her heart to do, and embrace her and my great-granddaughter, Savannah, as a new life for the Founteneau family and the citizens of St. Michel. The two will be formally presented at the annual St. Michel New Year's Eve state ball, which will celebrate its one hundredth year in just over two weeks."

As reporters from newspapers from all over the world began bombarding Sophie and the king with questions about the past, present and future, Sophie couldn't help but think that this was the very best revenge.

The Yves De Vaugirard PR nightmare was old news. Did he really think he could bring her down so easily?

A voice in the far reaches of her consciousness warned that the battle was just beginning.

Chapter Thirteen

"Oh. My. God. Sophie, is it really you?"

It was so good to hear Lindsay's voice. It had been nearly a month since she'd talked to her friend. Sophie settled into the deck chair on the terrace off her bedroom.

"It's really me, Linds. Merry Christmas Eve. I'm sorry to call so early, but I wanted to wish you a good holiday before the day got away from me." It was seven in the morning in Trevard, but Lindsay sounded wide-awake. "I wanted to call sooner, but…well, things have been a little crazy around here. How are you?"

"Are you kidding? I'm fine. I'm flabbergasted. You're a princess? I can't even comprehend it."

It was a beautiful day. In the low seventies, it was warmer than it had been, and compared to North Carolina in December, it was like spring. The sky was impossibly blue and the air smelled like a mix of herbs and sea salt. Sophie inhaled the delectable scent and reveled in the sound of her friend's voice.

"Yeah, you and me both. It's still a little surreal."

"It's been all over the papers and TV," Lindsay said. "I have to tell you that Mary nearly flipped when she heard the news. She's been acting like the two of you were tight. It's all I can do to keep from snorting. So you can see not much has changed. I have to get out of here. Know of any other countries looking for a princess?"

"Come for New Year's Eve, Linds. The king throws a big ball every year and this is our hundred-year anniversary. It would be fun. Plus I could really use some girl time right about now. I'll send you a plane ticket."

"I would if I could, but I just don't see how I can get away. But soon, okay?"

"I'm going to hold you to that. I've met someone and I want you to meet him."

She couldn't believe she was saying that. It was still too soon and with all the change that was swirling around her, there was no way to know where it was leading. Still, every time she doubted the relationship, Luc managed to prove her wrong. If anyone understood the crazy life that she'd fallen into, he did.

And frankly, she didn't want anyone else.

"Okay, so you get to be a princess and you get the hot guy. Not fair."

"Well, would it entice you if I told you that St. Michel is full of hot men?"

"Maybe…"

"Well, you'll just have to come and see for yourself. I'm not going to give up until I get you here."

They talked for a few more minutes about holiday plans, about how the issue of her illegitimacy could keep her from becoming queen—and how Luc had set his youngest brother Alex, who was an attorney, to comb the constitution for any sort of loophole that might help them change the law without unanimous approval of the Crown Council; and finally, Lindsay told her about how the police had finally ruled Laura's death an accident.

"A mechanical inspection they did showed that the accelerator on that old heap she drove stuck. That's what caused the crash. I thought you'd want to know."

Tears welled in Sophie's eyes and suddenly she wanted to bawl. On the one hand, Laura didn't commit suicide. It was a relief to know that after all that hard work and determination she didn't just toss in the towel. But on the other hand, it was heartbreaking that after Laura had come so far it all ended before she even had a chance to really spread her wings. The boys should've received the Christmas presents she sent them, alhough she knew all the money and gifts in the world wouldn't fill the void losing Laura left in their young lives.

"Linds, thanks for letting me know. I promise to call to wish you a happy New Year, okay?"

Then it was time to go. Adèle and her mother were coming for tea and then she and a delegation, which included Savannah, Luc, her grandfather, a few council members and Luc's brother, Henri, were going to deliver the toys to the St. Michel Community Center. Then they were all coming back to the apartment for a Christmas Eve supper. It was going to be a full day.

She was still sitting in the deck chair, holding her phone, when it rang again.

"What did you forget to tell me?" she asked, fully expecting it to be Lindsay calling back with a forgotten morsel of gossip.

"A better question is what did *you* forget to tell *me?*" The deep voice on the other end jolted her.

"Frank?"

"Hello, *princesse.* Why didn't you tell me your little secret before you took our daughter out of the country?"

The sarcasm in her ex-husband's voice set her teeth on edge. She did not have the time or patience to deal with him right now. She stood and walked back into the bedroom.

"I don't owe you any explanations. I followed the rules when I called and asked if you minded if Savannah came with me. You said you didn't mind. So it's all good. But I'm sure that's not the real reason you called. What do you want, Frank? Make it fast. I'm running late for an appointment."

"On Christmas Eve?" His tone was a bit gentler.

"Yes, on Christmas Eve. What is it?"

"Well, uh, I was just calling to say Merry Christmas."

Oh. She sat down on the bed.

"Well, Merry Christmas to you, too. How's Amber?"

Silence stretched over the line.

"You know with it being the holidays and all, I was just sort of missing you and that kid of mine. Where is she?"

Sophie hated herself for it, but she felt kind of bad for him. Not being able to see his daughter on Christmas. Even if it was his own choice to leave his family and move to the other side of the country for a woman who was closer to his daughter's age than his own. Sophie would've died if she had to wake up on Christmas morning and not see Savannah.

"She's not here right now." She was with a friend.

"Oh. Well, I guess I could call her cell. Is it working all the way over there in Europe?"

"Yes, it is. I think she'd really love to hear from you."

More silence. She got up and pulled the towel from her hair, then walked over to her dressing table and sat down.

"Uhh… I've been thinking about you, Soph. You know, missing you. Do you still think about me and what we had together?"

No. Now his melancholy was starting to make her squirm.

"Uhh…how would you feel about me coming out there for a few days? You know, maybe we could ring in the New Year together? You know, talk about being a family again?"

Okay. Now it was starting to make sense. Now that she was the *princesse* of St. Michel, she was attractive again. Or maybe he saw an opportunity to live the high life and wanted a piece of the action.

"No, Frank. I don't think that's possible. I've had a hard year. When you first left, I thought I'd never be whole again. But you know what? I healed. I've moved on."

She thought of Luc and how it felt to be in his arms, and a spiral of white-hot longing unfurled inside her.

"You can't keep my kid from me, Sophie." His voice was angry again.

"I don't intend to keep her from you. You can come and see her anytime you'd like."

"No. I want her to come home. She lives in the States and this is where she needs to be. Not in some backward foreign country."

"Frank, you didn't want her when she called to ask if you could come stay with her while I visited St. Michel. Do you expect me to believe you want her now?"

"Yeah, I do. I'll take legal action to get her back."

* * *

The staff had prepared a beautiful tea—scones, tea sandwiches, cookies and an array of fresh fruit. The spread was set out on the sideboard in the dining room. Sophie had given Adèle the day off—and Christmas Day, too. The staff who worked she'd made sure received double pay in addition to another paid day off—so that they could spend some quality time with their families. She hated to ask the woman to come in on her day off, but Adèle had heartily agreed to the Christmas Eve tea.

Sophie was eager to meet Marie, eager to glean the private bits and pieces about her mother that nobody except one who'd been there in the capacity that Marie had would know.

Marie did not speak English and Sophie's French wasn't good enough to communicate in St. Michel's native tongue. So Adèle had to act as a translator for her. This made her more determined to become fluent in the language.

"My mother was the one who informed the queen, God rest her soul, of Sylvie's pregnancy. She thought she was doing the right thing when she told. Though, now she wishes she had kept her mouth shut. That's why until now she remained quiet about the *princesse's* nuptials.

"Nuptials?" Sophie was so startled, she repeated the word to make sure she'd heard correctly. "As in marriage?"

Adèle nodded. "She didn't mention the *princesse's* marriage to the king after her death because he had made it clear that the *princesse's* relationship with Nick Morrison was a taboo subject. He was grieving and she couldn't bear to add to his torment. However, it saddens my mother to hear the press call Your Highness illegitimate, and she wants you to know that your parents were, in fact, married, even if it was after your birth."

Oh. It was *after* her birth. For a moment she'd thought she'd discovered the key to getting around the Crown Council. If she were legitimate, then their argument would be a moot point. Still…

"Thank you for sharing this with me, Adèle. It's not that I doubt your mother, but how is it that she knows they were married, when no one else does?"

Adèle repeated the question in French to her mother, and Marie talked animatedly, gesticulating as she spoke.

"She was with them. She accompanied Princesse Sylvie the night she and your father, Monsieur Morrison, ran away to St. Ezra. It is a *village perché,* er, a perched village." With her finger she traced a hill in the air. "You understand? An old medieval village, perched high upon a rocky hill."

"Yes, I know what you're talking about."

"St. Ezra is still very old-fashioned. Because of its location, it is virtually cut off from the rest of the world, and because of that, its people are usually cut off from news and those who might be celebrities. It was a place where the *princesse* and Monsieur Morrison would not be recognized. Because of that they went there to the *maire*—the village mayor—and exchanged vows in secret before boarding that ill-fated plane for Bora Bora that crashed and took their lives.

"My mother helped the *princesse* get ready for her wedding, but they wanted to go on their wedding trip alone. Thus her life was saved."

Marie had tears in her eyes as Adèle relayed the story to Sophie.

"She says, that time she decided not to tell the queen

because the last time she did, they sent the *princesse* away and she returned without her baby."

Marie gestured to Sophie and shook her head in a display of sorrowful regret before she resumed talking. Adèle said, "Although she often wishes she'd done something to stop the *princesse* from going on the plane that night. You see, my mother was to return to the castle before anyone got suspicious. She was not to go on the honeymoon to Bora Bora with your mother and Nick. Had she stopped her, maybe Sylvie would still be alive. She told once and it was wrong. She didn't tell a second time and it turned out tragically. She says many people admire you and the charity work you are doing. In your short time here, you have made a difference in the lives of many people."

The words took Sophie's breath, and she was moved nearly to tears. "Please tell your mother it's not her fault that things turned out the way they did. And I appreciate her sharing this information with me."

After Adèle translated Sophie's words for her mother, the older woman reached out and took Sophie's hand. Adèle's eyes widened, and Sophie understood enough of Adèle's words to know that she was admonishing her mother for touching the *princesse* like that.

"It's okay," Sophie said, holding on to Marie's hand.

A tear meandered down Marie's cheek, and she seemed visibly absolved of her guilt.

It was good to see Henri. His brother was one of the few men in the world with whom Luc could relax and let down his guard.

He'd convinced his brother to help distribute the toys

Sophie had collected, though it hadn't been a hard sell. With their busy schedules, it seemed there was never enough time to catch up. This drive to the castle, where they would meet Sophie, Savannah and King Bertrand, was one of those rare opportunities.

Henri shook his head at his brother's recap of what had gone on behind the scenes prior to the press conference— about the threats he'd heard the De Vaugirards tossing about and how the *vicomte* had set up Sophie.

"Ah, the political minefield you are forced to navigate," Henri said. "I'm glad the artifacts and antiquities I deal with don't involve the curmudgeons of the council."

"Right, except when you procure the loan of a priceless Monet—" Luc smiled "—and remind the council your job has some significance."

Henri shrugged. "I suppose getting my hands on a priceless painting pales in comparison to your bringing home a new *princesse.* But I'll have you know I had to cancel a mistletoe date with Raquel so that I could attend this soiree for your *princesse.*"

Henri was the ladies' man of the family. Happily single, he had a long list of women he kept in constant rotation, each more beautiful than the next. He was a master at juggling and somehow managing to keep each of them happy yet at arm's length.

"I'm sure Raquel will forgive you, since it's an official invitation from the king."

"Forgive me? I'll have to pay dearly." A wicked smile tugged at the corners of Henri's mouth. "Ah, but with Raquel, making up is always the best part. Even so, I would be remiss in my duty to state and family had I turned down the king's invitation."

From the castle, they would ride in the limousine with Sophie, Savannah and King Bertrand to the community center, where four of the seven members of the Crown Council had agreed to join them. The two De Vaugirards and Councilman Norbert Guillou had declined under the sour pretense of being otherwise engaged on this Christmas Eve— although it was perfectly clear their refusal was simply passive-aggressive backlash to the *princesse's* rising popularity.

"Besides, based on the photos I saw in the paper, I'm dying to meet Princesse Sophie," said Henri. "She sounds like my idea of the ideal—"

"Do not even venture where I think you are about to go," Luc warned.

"Oh, I see," said Henri. "Calling dibs, are we?"

You bet.

Luc slanted a quick glance Henri and steered his Audi A4 Cabriolet into a straightaway out of a serpentine turn.

"Your propensity for the inappropriate never ceases to amaze me."

"So what's going on with you, big bro?" Henri pressed.

What was going on? That was the million-dollar question. This time last month, he was just a man doing his job. Then he met a woman who turned him inside out.

Mon Dieu, what *had* happened to him? All he knew was he'd never felt this way about anyone. From that first day when he'd seen her standing there on the front porch of her modest little North Carolina house in that hideous big yellow coat, he'd fallen for her—it was her spunk, her tenacity and most of all her tendency to go against the grain of all things royal. She was authentic and sincere and just plain fabulous.

The perfect *anti-princesse*. He was so far gone it was becoming clear that he should simply stop fighting it.

"Okay, then… So…" Henri said as if he were reading his thoughts. "I approve, because all work and no play was beginning to make Luc a very dull boy. I can't remember the last time I saw you smile like that."

He hadn't even realized he was smiling. He raked a hand over his mouth, as if he could wipe the grin off his face. But it was hopeless. She did make him smile. She made him laugh and dream and feel things he thought he could never feel. Still, even as close as he and Henri were, he didn't feel like sharing the intimate details with him.

Fortunately for Henri, their stepmother's disgrace on the family didn't seem to have taken as big an emotional toll on him as it had on Luc. Henri dated frequently and always managed to keep his head above water and his public and private lives separate.

Luc had been cut a little deeper than his two brothers. Or maybe it was simply that he and his brothers were built differently. The three of them were as different as could be. Yet they'd always been close, and had grown even tighter since their father's death.

In the tumultuous sea of St. Michel politics, his brothers were a steadfast constant he knew he could count on, even if he didn't feel like kissing and telling.

The toy delivery couldn't have turned out better. They gave away five hundred wrapped presents to the children of the *Palais de St. Michel* staff and other families that needed help. Sophie was already contemplating how she could expand the holiday drive next year and provide festive food for families who might not have a traditional meal on their Christmas table.

Her grandfather assured her no one would go hungry. Still, if she and the Crown Council could enjoy an endless supply of expensive champagne throughout the year, the least she could do was to ensure that the people who served her were well fed and cared for.

After the issue of her legitimacy was settled, she planned to challenge the council to review staff wages. It was exhilarating to realize that she potentially held the power to create so much change. Nothing like the red tape and hurdles she had to maneuver when she worked for the county. That and the fact that Savannah was happy were reason enough to make her want to stay in St. Michel. Okay, so she had to count Luc in that list, too. The thought made her smile.

All that and she'd had the great opportunity to meet Henri, Luc's brother she'd heard so much about. While they were at the community center, and Sophie and Henri were working alone together giving out the toys, he mentioned that their youngest brother, Alex, was arriving later to surprise Luc for the holidays.

"It's the first Christmas we'll spend together since we lost our father," Henri said. "Alex just found out yesterday that he could get away and he decided to surprise Luc."

"Please join us for dinner tonight," Sophie insisted. "It's going to be informal. But I can guarantee that the food will be out of this world and the company will be divine."

"We would be delighted," he said.

She could tell that Henri was the charmer of the family. He just had a certain way about him, a perpetual spark of mischief twinkling in his brown eyes. He and Luc were alike in so many ways, yet so different.

She couldn't wait to meet Alex, to see the three brothers together. She'd grown up in a loving but small family. Because of that she always wondered what she'd missed as an only child and had always been fascinated by the dynamics of sibling relationships. The chance to glimpse the special bond Luc shared with his brothers made her giddy.

Once they were back at the apartment and everyone was busy toasting and sampling the hors d'oeuvres, she and Luc grabbed two flutes of champagne and stole away, alone out on the terrace.

"Carol of the Bells" played softly in the background, as the sun set over the Mediterranean Sea. A cool breeze swept in from the water blowing her hair across her cheek. Luc reached up and brushed the errant strand out of her eyes, then leaned in and dusted her lips with a whisper of a kiss. It felt like the world had shifted—her world had anyway. He just had that effect on her.

They were both careful about not being too physical in public. Nobody knew about them yet. Sophie didn't even fully know where they stood; they hadn't discussed it, but really there didn't seem to be a need. Everything felt…right. Everything from his voice, to his lips to the way his body felt against hers when he held her.

Theirs was a private slow burn rather than a flashing blaze. Even though the fire that smoldered between them was hot— so hot that sometimes it was hard to keep their hands off each other. Still, they wanted to be careful—in light of the near scandal with Yves.

The thought was a downer, and it made her recall the legitimacy issue, which made her think of the two things she needed to tell Luc—the conversation with Marie, and the phone call from Frank. She decided to start with the good news first.

"My chambermaid Adèle and her mother, Marie, gave me one of the best Christmas presents I could hope for," she said. "Stories about Princesse Sylvie."

She recounted how Marie used to be Sylvie's chambermaid, and she told Luc how Marie swore that her parents were married the day that they died in the plane crash.

"I was already born, so it doesn't help with the Crown Council battle. Too bad legitimacy isn't retroactive when the parents marry after the child's birth."

Luc's brows knit and a strange look passed over his face.

"What's wrong?" she asked.

"Nothing. Just realized something I need to check into. So, it must have been nice to hear firsthand from someone who knew your mother."

Sophie nodded, suddenly flooded with a warmth and a feeling of contented well-being, but it was short-lived as she remembered the other thing she needed to tell him.

"I also had a not-so-great experience today. My ex-husband called."

Luc's right brow shot up. "He did?"

"I don't really want to talk about him right now, because I don't want to spoil the festivities, but I thought you should know he's heard the *news*. I probably should've told him before I left. But there's usually no talking to the man. Today was no exception. He's threatening to cause trouble over Savannah living here. The perverse thing is he didn't have time for her when we were all in Trevard. Then it was next to impossible when he moved to California. I hate to sound cynical, but I think he's thinking in terms of child support. I get the feeling that he's thinking that now that my circumstances have changed, he'll sue for primary custody and get a hefty child-support check for his efforts."

She hated to sound so jaded, but after living with the man for fifteen years, sadly she knew that was how he operated. Always the opportunist.

"Don't worry about it," Luc said. "Especially not on Christmas Eve. Just know that I'll make sure he doesn't bother you."

"I don't want to keep Savannah from seeing her father. I wanted to warn you…just in case."

He pressed his forefinger to her lips.

"Don't worry. I will ensure that both you and Savannah are happy."

His words caused a lump to form in her throat. As if all the emotion she was feeling was lodged right there.

How did she get so lucky? Luc was clearly a huge part of the reason she wanted to stay in St. Michel. For once, everything seemed to be lining up and her heart was finally recognizing that he might be the one.

The one. For a perfect moment she stopped and savored the thought as Luc took her hand in his.

"Here he is." They flinched apart at the sound of the male voice behind them.

The look on Luc's face was priceless when he turned and saw Alex standing with Henri.

"Surprise, bro. Merry Christmas."

Alex was cut from the same dark, gorgeous Lejardin mold as his older brothers. Yet, as with Henri, she could immediately sense the differences. Maybe it was the contrast of his jeans, casual sweater and loafers next to the more formal attire of his older brothers or maybe it was the hint of a tan and the sun-bleached highlights that glinted in his longish mop of hair (no amount of money could buy hair color that perfect and Sophie's immediate impression of Alex Lejardin was that he was much too laid back to even contemplate hair color.)

"I don't believe it," Luc said as he enfolded Alex in a back-slapping man hug. "When did you get here? How did you know to come here?" Luc glanced from Sophie to Henri. "Wait a minute, I sense a conspiracy. Ah, but it doesn't matter. I'm so glad you're here."

Watching the three brothers together filled her with a bottomless sense of peace and satisfaction that carried her through the dinner and merriment.

After all the guests had gone home, Savannah went to bed anticipating a visit from "St. Nick." Even though Luc should've gone home to spend time with his brothers, he stayed to help her fill stockings for the staff and set out Savannah's Santa gifts. So Sophie and Luc set to work in front of the fire.

After they finished, he said, "I can't stay long, but I want a moment alone with you. It seems jolly old St. Nicholas entrusted me to give you a little something on this fine Christmas Eve night."

He produced a small, square box wrapped in gold paper out of his jacket pocket and handed it to her. Sophie's stomach flip-flopped as he handed it to her.

"He asked me to have you open it tonight." Luc winked at her.

She leaned in and kissed him.

"What a coincidence. He left something with me for you."

Sophie set the box on the coffee table and got up to retrieve a festively wrapped box from under the tree.

With another man, it might have been difficult to find just the right present or awkward to give it to him because their relationship was so new. And still so uncertain.

She sat down and handed it to him.

"Open yours first," he said.

She felt suddenly shy as she gently tore the paper from the box. "It's so beautiful, I almost don't want to ruin it."

Wasn't that the truth.

The phone call from Frank reminded her that they had married so young and been together so long. She'd had a few dates since they'd divorced, mostly with men she'd met waiting tables at the steak house, but she'd been so busy she hadn't had the time or desire to think of starting anything serious. Or maybe it was because no one had seemed worth the effort. Until now. Luc was a rare mix of sexy and sophisticated and he was just plain easy to be with. The first man to make her stop and think…maybe this could work…that maybe he could be the one. Even so, Frank was the only man she'd ever been with, and contemplating Luc as a lover was a bit overwhelming.

Frank had taken a lot from her when he'd left—literally and figuratively. He'd made her believe that love was a fairy tale that existed only in storybooks. But Luc made her want to believe in white knights and castles and happily ever afters.

As she lifted the lid of the box, the beautiful strand of gray pearls inside took away her breath. "Oh, Luc, they're beautiful."

"I'm glad you like them."

She slipped the pearls around her neck so that the clasp was in front and held up her hair so he could help her fasten them. "Do you mind?" she asked.

"My pleasure."

As he leaned in, his lips were a fraction away from hers. He was close enough for her to breathe in his breath and the intoxicating scent of him. After he slid the clasp into place, his fingers found their way around to the back of her neck, into her hair and he closed the distance between them.

Tender and soft, the feel of Luc's lips on hers sent heat shimmering through her body. His touch, the simple feel of his mouth on hers swept her away into a world that was theirs alone. Tonight things were different, deeper, impossibly right. And for the first time in a long time, her heart opened.

He shifted to deepen the kiss, the essence of him infusing itself in her senses, going to her head like rare and expensive wine. She was drunk on his taste, his scent, the feel of him so close to her. Her hands explored the expanse of his shoulders, trailed down the hard muscles of his back, and the shimmer of heat in her belly sparked and her yearning flamed, burning deep and hot.

"Luc, we have to stop," she murmured breathlessly as he trailed kisses down her neck. "We can't do this here. You warned me once that the walls have eyes."

"Your bedroom is totally blind," he whispered.

She wanted him. So badly. But right now it wasn't a good idea. Her life was taking so many twists and turns, she couldn't quite tell if making love to him would be a wrong turn. If it was, she might lose him forever, and she'd rather wait—as hard as that might be—than risk it.

Even though common sense screamed that the last thing

she needed was Luc in her bedroom, her heart answered that maybe that was exactly what she needed.

As if he sensed her dilemma, he stood and offered his hand. "Dance with me."

She laughed a shy laugh. "We don't have any music."

He held up a finger. *"Un moment, s'il vous plaît."*

He walked over to the stereo, which was still housed in the same antique armoire it had been all those years ago when Antoine lived here as a boy and Luc used to come over and hang out. Granted, the system had been upgraded with the latest state-of-the-art equipment in preparation for Sophie's visit, but everything was still in its original place, like an old friend in his corner.

"You seem to know your way around this place pretty well," Sophie said.

He scanned the impressive selection of CDs. "I spent a lot of time here, way back when. Prince Antoine was my friend and we spent many hours in this very room talking, laughing, listening to music."

"I didn't realize you were close with the prince." Her voice was soft and held a note of sorrow.

Luc nodded as he chose a Nat King Cole disc, set the CD to Play and pulled Sophie to her feet and into his arms. He didn't want to talk about Antoine. Not now—and he knew that's exactly how his friend would want it. He would've said go for the girl. Even if she was his niece, because he would've known Luc's intentions were pure.

As strains of "Unforgettable" emanated softly from the stereo, Luc decided he didn't want to talk, period. Not with words. He wanted to hold this woman in his arms and show her how he felt—connect with her, feel her body moving with his, lose himself in the feel of her and revel in the way she was responding to him.

It would be torture watching her dance with other men at the ball. He would be working, of course, and would have no time for dancing. Not when there was so much at stake. He pulled her closer, as if he could protect her with his body—surrounding her, coveting her, needing to make her his own. He savored the way she seemed to melt into him, fitting perfectly into the space he'd created for her, as if she belonged there. And she did. He knew that without a doubt.

She gazed up at him, her eyes dark and full of emotion, their lips a breath apart as they swayed together—not in a formal dance that moved them around the room, but in a slow, private dance of desire that moved through them, joining them, making them one.

When she'd entered his life, the moment he'd first set eyes on her, something had shifted. Life as he knew it had ceased to exist. It had gone from automatic gray, going-through-the-motions to something bright and shiny, filled with purpose and breathtaking possibility.

He hadn't looked back since that first day, and now that she was in his arms, he intended to keep moving forward—as fast as she would comfortably let him.

Chapter Fourteen

After Yves De Vaugirard threatened King Bertrand the morning of the press conference, Luc was successful in planting informants among the wait staff in the de Vaugirard households. From those plants, he obtained information that they were, indeed, plotting an attempt on the king's life. The plan was to be carried out at the New Year's Eve ball.

With this information, Luc tried to dissuade the king from holding the ball.

Granted, the party was only two days away, but this was a code-red security concern. It could cost the king his life, not to mention the danger it put Sophie and Savannah in. Informing King Bertrand of the traitorous information he'd uncovered involving his godson and good friend was one of the worst moments of Luc's life—ranking right up there with his father's death. The look of betrayal was heart wrenching. But it finally hardened into a stance of challenge

The king leaned back in his desk chair. "I will not cancel a hundred-year tradition. If I do it, it will appear as if I'm running scared. I refuse to live that way. I want them to understand I am the king and I will not buckle to pressure even if it costs me my life."

A silent understanding passed between them and at that very moment, Luc had never respected any man more in his life—nor had he known one so maddeningly stubborn.

"It is one thing to arrest the De Vaugirards for plotting to kill me," the king said. "But they are slippery and rich and short of your catching them with a smoking gun in their greedy hands, the likelihood that they will wriggle out of the plotting charges is great. But if we catch them in the act, it will be quite another matter."

Luc ran his hands over his tired eyes. The weight of the matter had been keeping him up nights. When he did manage to sleep, nightmares of assassination attempts plagued his dreams. He wasn't able to stop the monsters from killing Prince Antoine, but he'd be damned if anything happened to the king or Savannah or Sophie.

No. He would take the bullet before he lost Sophie or anyone close to her.

"What you must understand, Your Majesty, is that in all likelihood, they're not going to be the triggermen. They will place themselves in obvious places so that there's no doubt of their alibis."

However, the information he'd obtained from the informants coupled with an actual assassination attempt would, in all likelihood, present enough evidence for a sound conviction. It was a huge risk, one that he was not at all comfortable with, but because the king was hell-bent on holding the ball, this could be his opportunity to put the De Vaugirards away for good. One thing they had in their favor was that the two were getting anxious—and that's when people slipped up. They'd waited patiently all these years, biding their time, spacing out the murders and executing them carefully so that they looked like accidents. Just when they thought they were nearly home free, the king pulled his long-lost granddaughter out of the woodwork.

Oh, to have been a fly on their wall after the luncheon when Sophie was introduced.

"The important thing is that you guard Sophie and Savannah with your life," said the king. "My life is secondary to theirs."

It was a touching display of grandfatherly love, but, "Your Majesty, with all due respect, if you're assassinated before Sophie's position is secured, there will be more lost than a hundred-year-old New Year's Eve tradition. The entire Founteneau dynasty will come to an end."

"That is why I have complete faith in you, Luc."

The king's use of Luc's given name caught him off guard.

"I know you have my granddaughter's best interest at heart." The king stroked his chin and regarded Luc contemplatively. "I've noticed you two seem to have developed an affinity for each other."

The blood in Luc's veins ran cold and he could hear it rushing in his ears. In an instant all sorts of possibilities flashed in his mind—ranging from how he would react if the king forbade him to be involved with Sophie to what he would say if the king brought up Patrices's inappropriate behavior

and asked if he hadn't learned a lesson—but this was different. It was true that Sophie outranked him by virtue of royal
blood. He was a commoner. A simple man. But St. Michel law
did not prohibit monarchs from marrying out of the royal gene
pool and that was the one glimmer of hope that he'd clung to.

"In case you were wondering," the king said with a certain
look in his eye, "I think the two of you would do a world of
good for each other. And if you were ever planning on asking,
I would certainly give my blessing."

Luc was on his way to see Sophie when his phone rang.
"Lejardin."

"Lejardin here, too." It was Alex. "I have some news that
I think will make you very happy—and could very well make
me a national hero, too. It's that good."

Luc stopped and scanned the empty hallway to assure he
was alone. He was.

"What is it?" he asked cautiously.

"Are you absolutely sure that Princesse Sylvie and Nick
Morrison were married before they perished in that plane
crash?"

His heart lurched. On Christmas Eve, when Sophie had
told Luc of the conversation with Princesse Sylvie's former
chambermaid, he'd thought he remembered something about
illegitimate children being legitimized after their parents'
marriage, but he hadn't know where to look it up. Since Alex
was the lawyer, and was helping them comb the constitution,
he'd asked him to check into it. Could it be…

"It's the word of a chambermaid, who says she was with
Princesse Sylvie on the day she married. I don't have the documents, but I know where to look for them."

"Well, you'd better get your hands on them fast. That's her ticket to the throne. Article 222 of the St. Michel Civil Code states in part: children born outside marriage are legitimated by the subsequent marriage of their father and mother."

She wasn't expecting Luc tonight. Savannah was at a sleepover—with a security guard in tow, much to her dismay, but she was learning that along with the cool wardrobe and great shoe collection, the life of a princess came with excess security baggage, too.

Sophie had a date with a good book and a nice hot bubble bath. Because Luc had been working overtime with security concerns about the New Year's Eve ball, she'd resigned herself to seeing him in fits and snatches until their January 2 date to go to St. Ezra.

She was soaking in a hot sea of bubbles when Adèle knocked on the bathroom door. "*Pardonnez-moi,* Your Highness, I hate to disturb you, but Monsieur Lejardin is here to see you and I thought you'd want to know."

Luc? Here? A rush of adrenaline pumped through her at the unexpectedness of his visit.

"Thank you, Adèle. Please tell him I'll be right out."

She scrambled out of the tub hastily swiping a plush towel at the water and bubbles dripping from her skin. Nervous energy coursed through her and she dressed hurriedly in a pink cashmere sweater and black slacks.

The sight of her made him catch his breath. He loved her best with no makeup. Just the way she looked right now, with wet hair and bare feet looking oh so touchable in the dim glow of the lit Christmas tree she insisted on leaving up until after the new year.

"Hello," he said. "I probably should have called before I stopped by, but I need to talk to you."

"No." She ran a hand through her damp hair as she walked toward him. "I'm glad you're here. Is everything okay?"

He blew out a breath, pacing himself.

"I have news and lots of it. Do you want the good news, the even better news or the best news first?"

She stepped back and shook her head, looking bewildered and impossibly gorgeous. "Start with the just plain old good news and work your way up from there, okay?"

"Okay. Now that I think of it, I hope you consider this good news," he said, backtracking. "I think it's good because—"

"What? Just tell me."

"Your ex-husband won't be bothering you anymore. We offered him a reasonable sum of money and we will pay for his flights and accommodations for him to visit your daughter four times a year. He seemed to think it was a fair settlement. In exchange, he is not to challenge you for custody. Does that sound okay with you?"

She nodded, her brows knit. "That was easy." She shrugged. "Yes, I guess that is good news. I just hope he'll keep up his end of the bargain and come visit his daughter. What's the *even better* news?"

"Come on, let's sit down." Luc took her by the hand and led her to the couch.

She looked at him skeptically. "You're sure this is good news?"

He smiled. "You be the judge. Alex called with the answer we've been looking for."

Her eyes grew large. "Are you saying what I think you're saying?"

He nodded and relayed the conversation he'd had with his brother. The only problem was that the offices of the St. Ezra *maire* were closed until January 2. He'd made a couple of phone calls and discovered the delay. "That means we have four days before we can put our hands on solid proof. I think it's best that we don't tell a soul until we have that document in our hands. With all due respect, I think it's best that we hold off mentioning it to His Majesty, too. I would hate to disappoint him if for some reason this turns out to be a wild-goose chase." As the reality set in, Sophie was stunned speechless.

That was fine. He couldn't talk, either, could only answer her with a kiss, drawing her into his arms, savoring the taste of her and the warmth of her body pressed against his. As he held her, the world melted away. The emotions that had awakened that first day made a final shift into place, as if the right key had finally been inserted into the lock that had held him stoically captive all these years. He wanted her. Needed her. There was no more denying, no more pretending or trying to contain his feelings.

The journey to her bedroom seemed the longest path he'd ever traveled, starting and stopping again and again to savor the feel and taste of her, unable to quench his desire for this woman who had captured his soul. When they finally reached her room, they stumbled through the doorway, pulling at each other's clothes, driven only by the burning need to get closer, closer, until their bodies joined as one.

His touch was possessive. She wanted him to possess her. Every inch of her. She pulled his shirt over his head, wanting skin on skin. Wanting to touch and be touched. Wanting his hands on her body in places that had ached for him for far too long. A little moan of pleasure escaped her as he removed her sweater. His hands slid down her bare back and cupped her bottom through her pants, pulling her in so that her body begged her to let the hardness of him find its way home.

It had been a long time since she'd allowed herself to fully want, to fully trust, but that was over now and all that mattered was how she needed this man. His need for her made her feel powerful and beautiful. Strong and desirable. As no one had ever made her feel before.

The rest of their clothes fell away and he walked her backward to the bed and laid her down, covering her with his massive body.

"I love you," he whispered. "That was the other thing I came to say."

At that moment she knew that not only had she fallen in love with St. Michel, but somewhere along the way she'd fallen in love with Luc, too.

She looked as if she'd stepped from a dream. Luc's stomach constricted with renewed desire as he gazed across the ballroom at Sophie in that ruby-red gown that so perfectly hugged those curves he'd taken to dreaming about on the nights he wasn't able to possess them. Too bad she was proving to be as stubborn as her grandfather when it came to matters of security.

From his post on the east balcony, he watched her as she stood alongside her grandfather, receiving guests, as regal as if she'd been raised in a Grand Ballroom. All around her women in designer gowns and fabulous jewels mixed with men in tuxedos. Yet Sophie stood out among the rest, outshone every woman in the room, and Luc's gaze kept tracking back to her.

Sophie Baldwin was born to be a *princesse*.

He remembered how she felt in his arms last night. How their bodies had fit together as if they were made for each other, how they'd moved together so perfectly. A rush of longing coursed through him and he knew he was in trouble. Tonight of all nights he had to keep his mind on the job.

It was crucial.

Just as he had tried to dissuade King Bertrand, he all but begged Sophie to bow out of the New Year's Eve ball. He'd leveled with her, told her it was just too dangerous. But like her grandfather, she refused to run and hide.

Luc didn't know if she was brave or foolish—either way, he loved her and couldn't stand the thought of losing her when they'd just found each other.

According to the informant, the assassin would strike at the stroke of midnight. Luc and Dupré had revised the security plan for the evening. As far as the Crown Council was concerned—specifically the de Vaugirards—the plan Luc had detailed at the meeting two days ago was the only plan: the king would ring in the new year on the east balcony, as was tradition. But in reality, King Bertrand and Sophie would leave the party just before midnight. The revelers would think they were on their way up to the gossamer-draped, gilded balcony, where at the very last minute, Dupré would discreetly roll out a lifelike mannequin into the king's spot and place another in a red dress identical to Sophie's toward the back of the box. The king's decoy was the one they used to divert the media. From a distance it looked quite realistic.

The only other change to the plan was that they'd kept Savannah at home and planned to reply that the child was under the weather if anyone inquired after her.

The evening was half over. The dinner had gone smoothly and Luc was fairly comfortable that if the assassin stuck to the plan the informant had detailed, they would be okay. What worried him were the remaining hours leading up to midnight when there would be so much movement on the dance floor. His entire security force was on high alert, stationed inconspicuously, watching for anything out of the ordinary.

Because somewhere out there in the sea of silk and jewels lurked a killer, and if that killer attempted to strike tonight it was the end of the road for the de Vaugirards.

But Luc vowed that the royal family would not suffer another tragedy.

As if the New Year's Eve ball—the final exam of her deportment lessons—wasn't enough to rattle her nerves, just toss in a few nasty rumors about an assassination and it was enough to make Sophie a wreck.

Not to mention, she wouldn't be able to dance with Luc tonight. As the Baron von Something-or-other—one of her many dance partners tonight—twirled and dipped her around the wooden dance floor, he just didn't compare. Luc was the only one she wanted to dance with, and she didn't want to be here if she couldn't be with him. Reflexively she scanned the room to see if she could catch a glimpse of him, but he was nowhere to be found. Invisible.

Still, she had no choice but to make the best of this. Since her grandfather insisted that the show go on—and he had made such a big deal that the ball was the time when he would present her and Savannah—who was she to disappoint him?

She was the heir to the throne, so dancing with men who smelled of mothballs and bad breath, making inane small talk with smug, privileged women, and shrugging off the occasional death threat were going to be a hazard of the job, right?

Perhaps. But she didn't have to like it, she thought as the music ended. She curtsied to the baron and exited the dance floor, politely declining invitations to dance the next waltz.

Still, she had to draw the line somewhere.

Actually she already had. She refused to endanger her daughter, who was just as happy to stay in when she found out there wouldn't be any kids her age at the party.

Tomorrow, Sophie decided as she took a seat at the table that was reserved for the king and his party, she would draw the next line—she would sit down with her grandfather and have a serious talk with him about this pissing match he was having with the De Vaugirards. Enough was enough. The men were killers, plain and simple, and they needed to be put in their place. If Luc had enough evidence to arrest them for plotting to kill the king, she was all for running with it. Even if they managed to wiggle out of the charges, wouldn't their mission be exposed and wouldn't that in itself be enough to keep them from making any future attempts?

It seemed like a no-brainer, but who was she to say—and why didn't anyone else see it except her, and possibly Luc? She was just tired—and it was not quite eleven o'clock. She still had a good forty-five minutes to go before she could leave.

Maybe she could fake a headache, which wouldn't be a total lie. These people wanted to talk to her only because she was the king's granddaughter. All they wanted to do was gossip about her legitimacy—or lack thereof—or who was wearing which designer, and whose jewels were borrowed or, better yet, fake. Her feet hurt and she didn't want to dance anymore.

She just wanted to find Luc and go home and take a nice long bubble bath and talk about their trip to St. Ezra—

Two gunshots and a chorus of screams rang out in the ballroom. In a flash, Luc appeared from out of nowhere, shielding her with his body.

As he hustled her off to safety, through the crowd she saw her grandfather sprawled on the parquet floor.

Thank God for bulletproof vests.

The king had worn one under his tuxedo, and it had saved his life. The force of the bullet hitting the vest was what knocked the frail old man off his feet. He escaped with only a mild concussion from hitting his head on the wooden dance floor.

The second bullet had most likely been meant for her. But Luc had saved her.

Two days later, as Luc drove Sophie to the village of St. Ezra, she shuddered at the thought of how tragically things would have turned out if the killer had chosen to aim for her grandfather's temple rather than his heart. From this perspective, it seemed reckless to have gone through with the ball— when they knew good and well that there was a valid safety concern—just so her grandfather could prove he wasn't a man who was easily intimidated. Yeah, he'd come very close to being a dead man.

As she watched the hilly farmland of southern France roll by out the window of Luc's Audi, it seemed a miracle that innocent bystanders weren't hurt in the fray, that someone else hadn't been shot or that people hadn't been trampled in the frenzy to get out of harm's way.

Only now did she realize that on the day of the ball, she

hadn't truly believed they'd been in danger—that someone would actually hire an *assassin* to shoot another human being for his own personal gain. Only now did the magnitude of the situation sink in.

This accidental princess role she'd been playing wasn't make-believe. It was serious business and she was in it— she'd dragged her daughter into it—up to her eyebrows.

The only consolation—if it could be called a consolation—was that the authorities had arrested the gunmen and the Comte De Vaugirard at the ball. As far as Sophie was concerned, he could rot in hell, because that's where he belonged.

The bad news was his son, the *vicomte,* had escaped— throwing his father to the lions. With him loose, it was like a horror movie come to life, not knowing when the monster was going to pop up. She hated horror movies. She just wanted to go home. She wanted to wrap herself in that hideous mustard-yellow coat and disappear into the anonymous life she'd been plucked from just a month ago.

Luc reached out and rubbed her thigh. "Are you okay?"

"I don't know if I am or not, Luc. They actually tried to kill my grandfather, and I don't know if this is the kind of life I want to live."

"Everything is going to be okay. You're just a little shell-shocked by what happened."

Anger bubbled up inside her. *Shell-shocked?* As if it was something natural she'd get over. That made her *so* mad.

"How can you say that?" Her voice had an edge.

He slanted her a glance and returned his gaze to the road without answering her.

And *that* made her furious. Furious at him for being a part of this self-absorbed royal society. Furious at him for bowing to the whims of her grandfather when he knew the safety concerns—furious at him for…for…. She looked at his profile and her heart turned over in her chest. It wasn't because he was so devastatingly gorgeous.

It was because he was involved in all the things that made her so mad, yet he was so removed from them. Her common sense screamed at her that he didn't have a choice but to go along with the party, that he was just doing his job—and he did it well.

She and her grandfather were alive, weren't they?

Off in the distance, the *village perché* of St. Ezra rose like a giant specter on the horizon. Up there was the key to her future, although she might not need it once the Crown Council had a chance to reconvene and decide how to move forward without the De Vaugirards. But that didn't seem to matter anymore.

"Luc, come back to North Carolina with me."

This time he didn't look at her—he kept staring straight ahead at the road. "I'm not cut out for this life. Let's just stop. I don't want to go to St. Ezra. I just want to get Savannah and go home."

He pulled the car over along the shoulder of the road and sat there for a couple of beats before he looked at her. His eyes, his expression were devastating. "You're upset and that's understandable, but people are counting on you. I am counting on you. If you run away, you will be running from the truth, and taking away all that right and good and just from the people of St. Michel and essentially turning it over to those like the Vicomte De Vaugirard. If you don't stand up to evil, it will win."

Oh, God. Wasn't that, in so many words, what she used to

tell her clients? If they didn't face the hard times head-on, they'd never get to the good on the other side.

They drove the rest of the way to St. Ezra in silence.

They parked at the base of the hill and prepared to make the big climb up the steep incline to the top of this perched village—the place where her mother had run off to all those years ago to risk everything, to marry the man she loved so that she could get her baby back. So that they could be a family.

Didn't she owe it to her mother—and her daughter—to stand up and fight for what was right?

Gazing up at the village walls, she realized the situation was so much bigger than her, the only way she could approach it was to not think about making it to the top. She just needed to take the next step. And then the next. Tears welled in her eyes. She reached out and took Luc's hand and they took that first step together. Until they rounded about halfway up the hill and stood face-to-face with the Vicomte De Vaugirard, who was pointing a gun at Sophie's forehead.

In the off-season, no one but the locals came to St. Ezra. It was inland and just far enough north that the bitter winter winds left their biting mark on those who ventured up the hill. Luc knew he had to think fast to find a way to get the gun away from De Vaugirard before the homicidal maniac decided to use it on Sophie. The thought of that made him burn with anger, made him want to rip the gun right out of the bastard's hand and turn it on him.

The *vicomte* yanked Sophie toward him, pulled her in front of him and pointed the gun at her temple. She let out a scared squeak.

"If you scream, I swear I will blow your head off right now. Not that anyone would hear you, they're so far up there." Yves gestured upward with his head. Luc could tell by the crazed look in his glassy eyes that the *vicomte* would shoot. He said a silent prayer that Sophie didn't try to play the heroine. "Lejardin, turn around and start walking down the steps. Go on! Do it. *Vite!*"

Luc's heart hammered in his chest as he complied. Keeping his head forward, he scanned the area with his eyes, but all he could see was brown rock wall to his left and the long stretch of highway they'd traveled, which was visible over the low portion of the winding wall on his right. He didn't have much time to think of something and he'd have to act fast once he did. Because he was walking in front of Yves and Sophie, the madman could easily shoot him in the back of the head and leave him for dead.

"Why are you doing this, *vicomte?*"

"Don't talk, just keep walking."

He was taking a big chance of annoying him if he continued to talk, but right now, it looked as if that might be his only way out. The guy wasn't in his right mind—if he ever had a *right mind.* Getting him to talk was the best way to distract him so that he could knock the gun out of his hand.

But he'd only get one chance at it….

"I just don't understand why a man like you, someone who has everything would do something like this. Especially when Sophie was just telling me she has no desire to succeed her grandfather."

Silence.

Good. That meant Yves was thinking.

"She was saying she misses North Carolina and wants to

go back. Can't imagine herself here. So why don't you just let us go? You can go back to St. Michel, the Crown Council will carry on with their plan to name you as the king's successor and life will resume as planned."

Luc's mouth was so dry, he could barely form the words.

"Right, are you kidding me? They've put my father in jail."

"Then he needs you to set him free. As the future king, you have that power."

"I've worked long and hard waiting to become king."

Yes, there it was. Luc didn't say anything, in hopes that Yves would keep talking.

"There were so many of you in my way. But after Sylvie died, I got the idea, why not help them along. Celine and Thibault's accidents were a breeze." Yves made a sound as if he was blowing out a candle and white-hot anger from the injustice of the killing gripped Luc. So he'd been mostly right about the deaths, and the murderer had a gun to the head of the woman he loved. He had to steel himself to keep from acting irrationally. As they rounded the bends on the spiral, Luc could see Yves in his peripheral vision. He was getting lost in the story. The gun was not always at Sophie's temple. His hand was unsteady and on the steps down, it bounced up a little. It would take only another moment....

"Prince Antoine and his family, that was another story. So many of them. Like rats. And what's the best way to get rid of rats? You burn them all—"

As they rounded the next bend and Yves started to step down, the gun wavered a bit. In one swift motion Luc reached back and grabbed Yves's wrist.

"Run!" he screamed channeling all the crushing rage he

felt at the murder of his friend and the danger Sophie had been in into the vice grip he had on De Vaugirard.

Sophie tried to run back up the steps—it was the only way she could go since Luc, as he struggled with the gun, blocked the downward passage. Plus help was up toward the village. But before she could get away, Yves caught a fistful of her hair and held on as he continued to fight with Luc for the gun. She yanked backward. Yves lost his footing, stumbled on the steps and let go. Just as she started to run, the gun went off and Luc dropped to the steps in a puddle of blood.

It was the shock of seeing the man she loved lying in a crumpled heap that made her do it. Her loathing of the Vicomte De Vaugirard fueled the force. She turned around and head-butted the *vicomte* so hard that he fell backward over the low portion of the winding wall, into the mucky retaining pond. That's where the police found him when they arrived a few moments later responding to a report of gunshots.

Epilogue

Once upon a time, in a kingdom far, far away, there was a *princesse* who fell in love with a very brave man. It wasn't just his good looks that attracted the *princesse*—nor the fact that he resembled Olivier Martinez, only better. No, it was his knack for rescuing her that did it. And after she got used to the idea, she found it kind of sexy.

The king also thought his granddaughter *princesse's* love was a very brave man and he named him a national hero and knighted him a Chevalier of the Order of St. Michel.

The knight was never afraid to step up when it mattered. He stood by the *princesse* and her family through the best and worst of times. The brave knight even took a gunshot to the shoulder for his beloved *princesse* and survived to tell about the scar.

If that wasn't love, the *princesse* knew there surely wasn't such a thing.

Once the bad guys were tried and convicted of a slew of charges—including murder, attempted murder and treason, among other crimes—it became clear that the brave knight might not have to rescue his *princesse* that often—not from danger, anyway.

So the brave knight took her back to the *maire* of St. Ezra to complete the task of finding the papers that legitimized her birth. Being such a noble knight—and a very romantic soul— he proposed to the *princesse* in the same place where her parents had exchanged their wedding vows.

The *princesse* accepted the proposal with great joy, for she knew all along that he was more than just a brave knight. He was her prince.

And together they started planning their happily ever after. Because there's nothing like a royal wedding to raise the monarchy's approval rating.

* * * * *

Here's a sneak peek at
THE CEO'S CHRISTMAS PROPOSITION,
the first in USA TODAY *bestselling author*
Merline Lovelace's HOLIDAYS ABROAD *trilogy*
coming in November 2008.

American Devon McShay is about to get the Christmas surprise of a lifetime when she meets her new client, sexy billionaire Caleb Logan, for the very first time.

Silhouette
Desire

Available November 2008

Her breath whistled out in a sigh of relief when he exited Customs. Devon recognized him right away from the newspaper and magazine articles her friend and partner Sabrina had looked up during her frantic prep work.

Caleb John Logan, Jr. Thirty-one. Six-two. With jet-black hair, laser-blue eyes and a linebacker's shoulders under his charcoal-gray cashmere overcoat. His jaw-dropping good looks didn't score him any points with Devon. She'd learned the hard way not to trust handsome heartbreakers like Cal Logan.

But he was a client. An important one. And she was willing to give someone who'd served a hitch in the marines before earning a B.S. from the University of Oregon, an MBA from Stanford and his first million at the ripe old age of twenty-six the benefit of the doubt.

Right up until he spotted the hot-pink pashmina, that is.

Devon knew the flash of color was more visible than the sign she held up with his name on it. So she wasn't surprised when Logan picked her out of the crowd and cut in her direction. She'd just plastered on her best businesswoman smile when he whipped an arm around her waist. The next moment she was sprawled against his cashmere-covered chest.

"Hello, brown eyes."

Swooping down, he covered her mouth with his.

Sheer astonishment kept Devon rooted to the spot for a few seconds while her mind whirled chaotically. Her first thought was that her client had downed a few too many drinks during the long flight. Her second, that he'd mistaken the kind of escort and consulting services her company provided. Her third shoved everything else out of her head.

The man could kiss!

His mouth moved over hers with a skill that ignited sparks at a half dozen flash points throughout her body. Devon hadn't experienced that kind of spontaneous combustion in a while. A *long* while.

The sparks were still popping when she pushed off his chest, only now they fueled a flush of anger.

"Do you always greet women you don't know with a lip-lock, Mr. Logan?"

A smile crinkled the skin at the corners of his eyes. "As a matter of fact, I don't. That was from Don."

"Huh?"

"He said he owed you one from New Year's Eve two years ago and made me promise to deliver it."

She stared up at him in total incomprehension. Logan hooked a brow and attempted to prompt a nonexistent memory.

"He abandoned you at the Waldorf. Five minutes before midnight. To deliver twins."

"I don't have a clue who or what you're..."

Understanding burst like a water balloon.

"Wait a sec. Are you talking about Sabrina's old boyfriend? Your buddy, who's now an ob-gyn doc?"

It was Logan's turn to look startled. He recovered faster than Devon had, though. His smile widened into a rueful grin.

"I take it you're not Sabrina Russo."

"No, Mr. Logan, I am *not*."

* * * * *

Be sure to look for
THE CEO'S CHRISTMAS PROPOSITION
by Merline Lovelace.
Available in November 2008 wherever books are sold,
including most bookstores, supermarkets, drugstores
and discount stores.

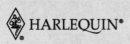

HARLEQUIN®

American ★ *Romance*®

Laura Marie Altom
A Daddy
for Christmas

The State of Parenthood

Single mom Jesse Cummings is struggling
to run her Oklahoma ranch and raise her
two little girls after the death of her husband.
Then on Christmas Eve, a miracle strolls onto
her land in the form of tall, handsome bull
rider Gage Moore. He doesn't plan on staying,
but in the season of miracles, anything
can happen....

**Available November
wherever books are sold.**

LOVE, HOME & HAPPINESS

REQUEST YOUR FREE BOOKS!

2 FREE NOVELS PLUS 2 FREE GIFTS!

♥ Silhouette®

SPECIAL EDITION®

Life, Love and Family!

YES! Please send me 2 FREE Silhouette Special Edition® novels and my 2 FREE gifts (gifts are worth about $10). After receiving them, if I don't wish to receive any more books, I can return the shipping statement marked "cancel." If I don't cancel, I will receive 6 brand-new novels every month and be billed just $4.24 per book in the U.S. or $4.99 per book in Canada, plus 25¢ shipping and handling per book and applicable taxes, if any*. That's a savings of at least 15% off the cover price! I understand that accepting the 2 free books and gifts places me under no obligation to buy anything. I can always return a shipment and cancel at any time. Even if I never buy another book from Silhouette, the two free books and gifts are mine to keep forever.

235 SDN EEYU 335 SDN EEY6

Name	(PLEASE PRINT)

Address	Apt. #

City	State/Prov.	Zip/Postal Code

Signature (if under 18, a parent or guardian must sign)

Mail to the **Silhouette Reader Service:**

IN U.S.A.: P.O. Box 1867, Buffalo, NY 14240-1867
IN CANADA: P.O. Box 609, Fort Erie, Ontario L2A 5X3

Not valid to current subscribers of Silhouette Special Edition books.

**Want to try two free books from another line?
Call 1-800-873-8635 or visit www.morefreebooks.com.**

* Terms and prices subject to change without notice. N.Y. residents add applicable sales tax. Canadian residents will be charged applicable provincial taxes and GST. Offer not valid in Quebec. This offer is limited to one order per household. All orders subject to approval. Credit or debit balances in a customer's account(s) may be offset by any other outstanding balance owed by or to the customer. Please allow 4 to 6 weeks for delivery. Offer available while quantities last.

Your Privacy: Silhouette is committed to protecting your privacy. Our Privacy Policy is available online at www.eHarlequin.com or upon request from the Reader Service. From time to time we make our lists of customers available to reputable third parties who may have a product or service of interest to you. If you would prefer we not share your name and address, please check here. ☐

SSE08R

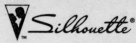

COMING NEXT MONTH

#1933 THE COWBOY'S CHRISTMAS MIRACLE
—RaeAnne Thayne
The Cowboys of Cold Creek
Widow Jenna Wheeler vowed to make this the best Christmas yet for her four young children. But Carson McRaven, the arrogant multimillionaire who bought her family's ranch, was the wildcard—would he be the Grinch who stole Christmas...or the cowboy who stole Jenna's heart?

#1934 HER FAVORITE HOLIDAY GIFT—Lynda Sandoval
Back in Business
When attorney Colleen Delany took on a wrongful termination lawsuit, she hardly expected to come up against her old law school nemesis Eric Nelson. There probably wouldn't be a meeting of the legal minds between the two opponents, but soon a meeting under the mistletoe seemed inevitable....

#1935 THE CHRISTMAS SHE ALWAYS WANTED
—Stella Bagwell
Men of the West
When Jubal Jamison took the job as veterinarian at the Sandbur ranch, he was surprised to find former flame Angela Malone working there, too. But this wasn't the only surprise in store for him this season—for the woman he'd almost married eleven years ago had a secret to share with him...just in time for the holidays!

#1936 THE MILLIONAIRE'S CHRISTMAS WIFE
—Susan Crosby
Wives for Hire
Entrepreneur Gideon Falcon had an idea that would make him a fortune. But to look legit to investors, he needed a wife and stable home life. Temp agency owner Denise Watson agreed to provide the front, but would their very real attraction for each other get in the way of business?

#1937 IT'S THAT TIME OF YEAR—Christine Wenger
The Hawkins Legacy
...The time of year widowed mother Melanie Bennett couldn't stand. Last year, she lost her husband in a winter storm, and still blamed emergency relief manager Sam LeDoux for not doing more. But this year, forced into close proximity with Sam at the Snow Festival, the healing—and the loving—began....

#1938 AND BABY MAKES FOUR—Mary J. Forbes
Home to Firewood Island
Charter pilot Lee Tait had finally gotten her life back in order when an unexpected pregnancy threatened to clip her wings. Then she met Rogan Matteo. Rogan, with seven-year-old in tow, was searching for second chances, too. Soon his passion for Lee took flight. But were they in for a crash landing?

SSECNM1008BPA